A VIEW FRO

Paul Toolan was born in northern England but now cheerfully admits to being a southern softie living in rural Somerset. After a rewarding career in Further Education and Universities he wrote books/lyrics for musicals before 'turning to crime'.

A Killing Tree and *A January Killing* are the first of the Detective Inspector Zig Batten series, rural noir crime novels set amongst the apple-orchards of England's West Country. The third, *An Easter Killing*, will be out soon.

Paul's first collection of short stories, *A View from Memory Hill* gives voice to the thoughts and dilemmas of mostly older minds, whose common ground is the half-shaded landscape of memory.

Like Zig Batten, Paul enjoys walking, gardens, fishing and a whisky or two. Unlike him, he enjoys cricket and the taste of mushrooms and loves travelling to sunnier climes - Greece and Crete in particular.

A View from Memory Hill

Stories 'of a certain age'

Paul Toolan

Published by Paul Toolan

Original cover photo by kind permission of Peter Toolan.

Introduction

We live life forwards, but understand it backwards. It's a personal journey, either way.

In *Memory Hill* and *At Yeovilton Weir*, Maeve helps Jack, her Alzheimer's husband, revisit the past in a search for understanding. Theirs and other voices here, are 'of a certain age', their common ground the journey into half-shaded landscapes of memory.

Younger voices are heard too, in stories uplifting and regretful, ironic and sinister, optimistic and questioning.

Will *Ruby, the Silver Surfer* learn to cut and paste and save?

Should *Billy the Quid* sell up?

Why is Lydia *Sleepless in Southampton*?

Can Frank Smith cope with being an *Old Man in a Young Pub*?

'What's in your bag, mister?' asks the small boy in *A Bag for Life*.

See for yourself…

Table of Contents

Memory Hill

A slow climb.

The slowest ever.

Twenty stuttering minutes and not half-way. In 1961, they climbed Ham Hill in less than ten because she'd challenged him to a race.

'I let you win,' he said, eyes smiling, as they drank in the vast view of Somerset from a bench on the hill's peak.

How young were they, that first time? Eighteen? Nineteen? Now, Jack wanted to give up, go back. But Maeve would get them to the top, before sunset.

'They've made it steeper,' he said, leaning on his walking-pole. 'First time we climbed it, in…in…'

'1961', Maeve said.

'Was it? Well, it's steeper now.'

Ham Hill was the same, but she wouldn't risk saying so. 'Ready?' she asked.

No reply. His walking-pole slipped from his fingers to the grass. These days, he insisted on calling it a *stick*, if he called it anything. She checked his eyes. Yes, drifted again. She moved across his vision to bring him back.

'*What*?'

'Ready to go on?'

'Where?'

Maeve bit her tongue. She pointed. 'There. To the top.'

'Top of *what*?'

Patience, Maeve. 'Top of Ham Hill.' *Our* hill.

'What for?'

She smiled at him. Occasionally, it worked. Jack's feet stayed put. She picked up the pole, wrapping his fingers round the handle.

'For the memories', she said, easing him forward, thinking back...

*

Her forgetfulness was tiny, compared to Jack's. She'd ushered him from their GP to the hospital and home again. When you're a child, it's tests at school. When you're older…

Whatever the test, Jack failed. She had to look up 'chronic', because she'd forgotten what it meant. 'Worsening with time', the dictionary said. Her GP was kind, clear.

'Alzheimer's is a rocky ride. Enjoy being together, yes? I mean, for as long as Jack remembers you?'

Jack was sleeping, on the day-bed she'd rigged up in the conservatory. When he was bad, any sleep would do. She was Jack's dictionary now, non-stop, exhausting - the reference book for all the people, all the objects he could no longer name. The butt, too, of each resulting outburst.

'Do you know *nothing*?' he would yell. '*Nothing*?'

She did her best to empathise. When even a simple

word refused to flip from her own mind to her tongue she felt…what?

Like she was reaching for, say, a cookbook in the kitchen, but it's gone. So, you fetch it now from the cupboard under the stairs. Next time, it's not there at all, but *up*stairs, on the landing. And soon, before you know it, you're searching through a junk-pile in the loft. Nine times out of ten you trudge back down, with nothing in your hand or on your lips.

How worse was it for Jack? His memory's flown higher, from loft to roof, she thought. Climbed a hill. Scaled a mountain.

What's the difference between a mountain and a hill? she asked herself. You see? Can't remember. Jack was still asleep. She switched on her tablet, and searched online.

'Disputed', said the World Wide Web. A mountain *used* to mean a bump above a thousand feet or more. A hill was lower.

Not now. 'Other factors' have come into play. She scrolled down.

Steepness was one.

Terrain another.

She pulled a face and closed the tablet. Who are these self-appointed know-it-all's? If they dropped in now, to our conservatory, would they tell me, oh, no, no, it's not a mountain Jack has to climb, to remember where he put the stamps he bought last week.

It's just a tiny hill.

She looked through the window at the honey-brown,

green-clad slope of Ham Hill, at its War Memorial steepling into cloud. Ham Hill was the reason they bought the house. People drive up there, for the bluebells, the view, the dog-friendly pub.

We don't, me and Jack. We walk, up the steep side, to keep us going.

And for the memories.

*

Jack stuttered to a halt again. She handed him a water-bottle, top removed. He stared at it. She folded his fingers round the bottle, and made him drink. From the corner of her eye, with horror, Maeve spotted their new neighbours - the Devil and his Wife, she called them - trotting their cloven hooves down the slope towards her.

Maeve once hid behind a parked car to avoid their condescension. *From Hell*, and unforgettable, no matter how hard she tried.

Their ill-trained devil-dog would nip her for fun. The dog leered at Jack. *Leered.* Jack hated the dog more than the neighbours. Even when he couldn't remember it, he hated it.

The track was too narrow to pass without acknowledgement, so small-talk opened its mouth, and gobbets of ingrained pretence dribbled out. Only Jack kept silent, eyes on the mean-minded dog.

'Struggling up the hill again, I see,' said Devil-Wife, false smile trowelled on. 'Why don't you use your common sense and drive, like the tourists do?'

No, Maeve said, unsmiling. We've lived here since 1963. We've walked up a thousand times. *Long before you were vomited from Hell to infest the house next door!*

The Devil poked the fire.

'*Boots*!' he snarled. 'Must have good boots.' He looked down his nose at Maeve's. 'Buy better boots,' he said, twiddling an expensive foot in her face, while balancing easily on the other. Young. Effortless. 'A solid platform. See?' He stamped his jackboot on the grass, crushing it.

Stay here much longer, Maeve, he'll demand to see your documents. *Oh, really?* she murmured.

Jack ignored both Devil and Wife. His eyes screwed into the circling dog, with its brimstone feet and hellfire jaws. Devil-Wife worked it, on a long lead. Maeve felt Jack's dangerous stick begin to twitch against her leg.

'Onwards and upwards,' she mumbled, diving into cliché to save the day. Jack was in Hell already. He could do without an unscheduled meeting with Satan.

But as she moved, so did the dog, teeth afire. The long lead snaked out, unravelling like an anchor chain. Jack's stick flicked up to defend, then across and down in anger. Maeve moved between Hell and her husband just as the anchor chain bit, and the dog's neck snapped back.

'Naughty *Pootsie*', cooed Devil-Wife.

'Fit as a butcher's dog! Haaarh!' bellowed Devil, the sudden movement his excuse to hit the down-slope.

Jack's stick hit the down-slope too, missing the dog and catching Maeve on the shin - muscle, not bone, thank god. But it stung. She cursed the Devil-spawn as they brimstoned away, leaving her with the makings of a mighty bruise. When she looked back, all three Devils looked back too, teeth out, laughing.

*

This time, it was Maeve who had to stop, her shin painful. She handed Jack an energy bar, breaking the wrapper for him. He fumbled it open and began to chew. She rescued the wrapper from the ground and popped it in her backpack. Before she could unwrap her own, Jack was slogging up Ham Hill, crumbs bouncing off his waterproof like hailstone.

At least he's going *up*, she thought - in the footsteps of the Ancient Britons, who did the same. Till the Romans marched up faster, through fire and fortifications, to kill and confiscate. Ham Hill commanded the landscape, its quarries yielding golden stone for Roman villas.

She and Jack had a modest hamstone villa at the hill's foot. But they didn't steal theirs. They took out a mortgage. In 1963. The same year sex was invented, according to Philip Larkin. He wasn't wrong, Maeve thought, watching a temporary Jack hammer his way to the hilltop. It's the sugar in his energy bar, she thought, laughing at the double-entendre.

Unwitting.

Like Alzheimer's.

When she limped to the peak, he was staring at a metal plaque mounted on a block of hamstone. Arrows engraved into the metal pointed to landmarks near and far. She traced her finger along an arrow marked 'Burrow Hill'.

'A lot easier climbing *Burrow* Hill, Jack? A thimble, compared to this?'

Jack peered at the arrow, following the thin line into the valley below, to a distinctive round bump with a single tree on top. They'd been there, many a time.

'Don't know it,' Jack said.

She'd learned not to disagree.

'Yes, Burrow Hill. A pretty little hill. And can you just make out Exmoor, way over there?'

He followed her finger, searching without and within, before shaking his head.

'Too far,' he whispered. 'Too far away.'

They gazed, in silence, at vague purple shapes in the distance. Then, without warning, Jack's stick jerked up in his hand, swung left and right, and fired at nothing. '*Glastonbury Tor!*' he shouted. '*There!*'

Maeve stilled him, gentle fingers on his arm. 'Yes, Jack. We've climbed that too.' They had. 'You can't see it from here.'

He scanned the horizon, scoured it, till the wind stung his eyes. When she tried to dab them with a tissue, he slapped at her hand.

'Too far,' he muttered, his stick waving at nameless bumps of landscape and swirls of sky.

'Too far away', voice a whisper again, stick dropping down, tapping vaguely against stone.

Is it the landscape that's too far away? thought Maeve.

Or memory? Or something else? You've reached the hilltop, and the reward is not knowing.

Jack himself was tramping towards the War Memorial. He could once recite all the war dead names engraved on the tall column, and point to his grandfather's name, rank and regiment, remembered there. These days, he read the names afresh, each visit. 'Brave young boys', he said, each time. 'Brave boys.' It calmed him.

Maeve kept an eye, easing her bruised leg onto 'their' bench, wood and metal, a crow's nest. Below, the A303 rumbled through a valley mottled with ancient trees and villages. Military lines of soft fruit and newly-planted orchards added structure. Her eyes tracked from one church tower to the next, each one an age-old marker of marriages and deaths.

Jack was standing behind her.

He tapped the bench with his pole. 'Where we met,' he said.

Almost true. Might today be a good day? They first met in the old Yeovil Library, in Hobbies and Leisure.

I was looking up long-distance walks. Jack too. We put our hands on the same book, at the same time, and our fingers touched. I thought it must be fate.

A rat-tat-tat of metal on metal broke her thoughts. Jack's stick was shaking, rattling against the stanchion of her favourite bench. She had no heart to still him.

Now, sometimes, it feels like chance. And little more.

The rattling increased.

The Ridgeway, that was the book. We dreamed of walking

it, even before it became a National Trail. We won't walk it now.

Jack bumped against the bench. 'Yes. Where we met', he said. 'Why we bought the house. Our house, there.'

They stared at rooftops, his silent stick pointing. The house wasn't visible from here.

'Ham Hill's a magnificent hill. Don't you think so, Jack?'

'Best hill in the world', he said, staring at the War Memorial, coloured now by specks of sun.

'Our bench, Jack. On our hill. Do you remember what we used to call Ham Hill?'

'Tuh. Course I do, Maeve. How could I forget?'

She smiled at her old Jack. On a different day, the same question might be answered with a scowl.

But, having sworn he remembered, Jack struggled to.

Maeve took his hand and drew him down onto the bench, to rest. The walking pole dropped once more to the grass, as Jack's frown swelled. He stared at the hill, shaking his head, slowly, then faster, sweat seeping from his brow. She dabbed it with a tissue, and he let her. After an aching pause, he peered at the bench. Then at Maeve. At the bench, again. At Maeve.

'I asked you to marry me. Here,' he said. His free hand, shaking, patted metal and wood.

Maeve mopped her eyes with the damp tissue, soaking it.

'Yes, Jack. It's why we gave Ham Hill our own special name. Remember?'

Jack's concentrated frown returned, eager, sharpening his brow.

But nothing came of it.

Shaking his head as if dislodging a fly, he struggled to his feet and tramped down the track, walking-pole forgotten on the ground. His boots ate up twenty yards before he realised Maeve was not beside him. She remained, a slumped figure, on 'their' bench, shredding the sodden hopeless tissue into tiny pieces.

'Hurry up, Maeve!' Jack shouted. 'It's downhill now! It's easy!'

Maeve laugh-cried, laugh-cried on the hilltop. Struggling to her feet, she retrieved Jack's stick, leaned on it, and limped after him. A white dust of shredded tissue floated away to nothing.

In sunset, they wobbled home together, down Memory Hill.

Ruby, the Silver Surfer

I'm 73, and he's asking, 'have you done your homework, Ruby?'

Nearly said, 'yes, sir, here, sir'.

Nearly didn't come back at all.

Ruby White ran her hand along the old school desk, like the ones at Primary when she was five. Welcoming, and clever, she had to admit, even down to the ink-well and graffiti.

Jenny loves Joe xxx, hers said.

She found the button Mike had shown them, at the very first class, and pushed it. With a whirr, the lid flipped back, and a shiny slim laptop emerged from its wooden cave. 'Schhhkk', it went, before settling on the desktop - a bit smug, she thought - a metal cherry on a scratched wooden cake.

Shiny and slim, Rube. Like you used to be.

The first time Mike showed them, he said, 'now that's what I call a desktop'. Dot Clarke, who used to work for the Pru, snootily explained the reference.

'Tell him not to say it again, Dot. I might have a stroke, laughing.'

Mike was standing over her.

Just her.

Ruby was in early, for 'one-to-one'. The others, it'll be tea and a raspberry flapjack in the college cafeteria.

Have I done my homework, indeed!

'I did', said Ruby.

It was half true. She'd cut-paste-saved the little document, and printed it. Once her grandson, Harry, had shown her how to load paper in the printer. And how to print. Harry was nine. But they'd cut-paste-saved at home, her home, where her daughter's old computer now resided. So, it *was* homework. Sir.

Mike looked it over.

She looked at Mike.

She once had a Michael of her own.

This one's more a Simon or a Wayne, she thought, swanning around in a T-shirt. When did they start putting words on T-shirts? Her pebble-specs couldn't make it out, and it was creased from Mike leaning over. *Manhatt*, it said. *Tradin Compan*. Must have bought it in America. He seemed the sort who'd risk a visit. Got those metal trousers in America too, because isn't that where Manhatt is? They weren't jeans. Black cloth like a bin-liner made of steel, held together with zips. Found herself looking at the obvious and wondering when button flies went out of fashion.

He's the student, she thought. And me, I'm the teacher, with my nice skirt and blouse, ironed, and a little jacket in case he flings open the windows again. Is it so whatever comes out of these computers doesn't poison us?

I put on a pair of Sketchers this morning, for comfort.

You never know, there might be pedals to push, like in a car. It's a case of just-in-case, with me. Him, Mike-Wayne-Simon, he's wearing half a red trainer and half a brown brogue, glued together. Yes, *I'm* the teacher.

I'm not though. It's College, and I nearly didn't come back.

First time, it took me two turns to find the room, despite the outsize *SILVER SURFERS* banner you could spot from Mars. I wear specs, yes, but who wants their thick lenses rubbing in?

'On time, again, Ruby. I like a keen student. And your homework's ace. Not bad for a lass who said she might quit?'

So, I'm ace and a lass now, am I? He's young, Ruby. Make allowances. Mike pushed the 'on' button on her laptop.

'It's slow today', he said, and she looked at the clock on the classroom wall. Like the reassuring desks, it was 'old-school', brown Bakelite, white face, old-fashioned hands. A pretend old-school chart, hanging from a posh nail, had pictures of computers and keyboards, and explanations in little boxes on the ends of arrows. Reminded her of Primary school. But no computers there in 1949, Rube, when you were five.

1949. *Gawd.*

Mike didn't mean the clock, of course. His young finger pointed at the widget on the laptop screen, a tiny clock-face with a spinning arrow. Like a little toy train on a circular track.

They both watched it now, as the computer booted -

watched it spin down and around, down and around, and begin again.

Starting up.

Winding down.

Starting up.

Winding down.

Janice, her daughter, made her join the class. Well, not 'made' exactly. Ruby did have a mind of her own. It was Graham, the son-in-law, who'd done the pushing. Got fed up of showing her how to use the bloody great computer-gubbins Janice gave her. Steady, Ruby. Bad language in class, tut, you'll get expelled. Ooh, there's a thought. But Mike was leaning over because the laptop had its boots on, or whatever he called it.

She was getting extra help. Mike knew she was a 'struggler'. Ruby knew it too. Because the staffroom door was open when she passed last week, and she overheard.

Nearly didn't come back.

'Now, Ruby, do you recall how to rename a document?'

'Why would I want to rename a document?' She nearly called him 'Sir', but they had to call him Mike. And he's a 'tutor' not a teacher. As if there's a difference.

'Well, if you want to progress from 'Starting Out' to 'Intermediate'...'

Did she want to? Snooty Dot Clarke was an Intermediate. 'We get a Certificate, you know, Ruby.' Rube wasn't sure about being Certified.

'How can I rename it if I don't know what it's for? I mean, what's going in it?'

'What would you like to go in it, Ruby?'

Why's he asking me? He's the teacher.

'Let's say the 'document' is a letter. A letter that you want to keep. If you name it, you can file it - and find it again. Is there anyone you need to write to?'

Write to. Hmph.

Write to.

Write.

With a proper pen, held in my fingers. Fingers are for wrapping round a pen, your own flesh and blood guiding the ink, loops of letters bleeding from your heart onto white paper, folding the page, sealing the envelope.

Ruby tasted glue on her tongue, from old stamps, long ago. She saw a red post-box and her young fingers sliding in the letter. After she'd kissed it. And the postman collecting hers and all the others, then days later, a week, more, another letter coming through her letterbox and unsteady fingers opening it, sitting on the old garden bench in morning sunlight, and reading what it said.

Breath held.

Her tea untouched.

The needy cat un-stroked.

And the bright flowers twisting into dark useless weeds as a wind not forecast blew the envelope from her loose white hand into the shrubbery.

The official print was large enough to read, her eyesight never good, even then.

Ministry of Defence, it said.

And the letter in her hand was two letters. Theirs. And

hers. The one she'd posted not two weeks ago. Michael never got to open it. The letter from the Ministry was kind in tone. But the words, well.

'No. Not a letter,' she said. 'Something else.'

*

Mike was opening photos, on a laptop screen. The other Silver Surfers followed every word, but Ruby was, yes, a struggler. And she had a photo album in her bedroom, in the dressing table drawer. When she couldn't sleep, she'd open it and stare at memories. No need to plug it in and put its boots on, or whatever he called it. Why put memories on a laptop screen?

Easy to store and share, Mike was saying. He showed them how to send a photo from one Silver Surfer to another, there, in the pretend-old-fashioned-classroom. Ruby still took hers to Boots the Chemist. Well, Janice did. On something called a stick. A memory stick.

*

The College caff did a decent cup of tea. They sat together, the whole class, sipping out of plastic cups. Dot Clarke said the place was like a works canteen, stuck-up cow. Ruby preferred the tea-break to the class. *Tea*, you can understand.

'Are you attending next week, Ruby?' asked Dorothy Clarke. She disapproved of abbreviation, so Rube always called her Dot. 'I was not convinced you'd venture back. Given your previous proclamation.'

Ruby had said the classes made her feel like a machine. Still did. She sipped her tea, and glanced at the 'Toilet' sign.

'Must dash, Dot,' she said, escaping down the corridor.

In the Ladies, at the sink, she scrubbed her hands. How many times today, Rube, and it's only two-fifteen? It could have been Dot Clarke in the mirror. 'Attending next week, Ruby?'

I might. I could cut-and-paste-and-save something.

Her tea was cold when she sat back down. Dot was rabbiting on about Email. Dot was a *Non*-Struggler.

'We emailed each other, there and then in the classroom. Myself, Jenny, Rose and Faye. It was extremely exciting.'

You could've just turned your necks and said hello, thought Ruby.

Or sent a letter.

'Having family in Australia, I could be on the telephone all day.' With a dry laugh, Dorothy Clarke corrected herself. 'All *night*, I mean. But with Email, time is irrelevant. And so very useful for sending *detail.* Aeroplane itineraries and the like. We fly to *Oz* three times a year, you know.'

Aeroplanes. A flight. A military flight. Ruby's cold tea was the untouched tea in the garden and her canteen chair the garden bench and she held not a paper napkin in her hand but a letter, drawn like a sword from the official envelope which blew into the shrubbery, and lay there like a white flower on a grave.

'Detail, yes,' mumbled Ruby.

'Mike intends to teach us Skype,' Dorothy droned. '*Most* exciting. It's an on-screen telephone call, a two-way video conversation with the other side of the world. Imagine that? Seeing my new grandson, ten days old, through the magic of technology!' She raised her plastic cup, pinkie in the air, admiring the silence.

Waiting for applause, Ruby thought, but Dot was off again.

'You, Ruby, are more fortunate than I. Yours lives a mere *bus* ride away.' Ruby couldn't drive. And didn't Dot know it. '*Your* grandson can be handed back the instant you grow tired of him.'

Ruby wanted to spit in Dot's face, *I never grow tired of him!*

Because after I hand him back, the house is a morgue.

*

Next, Mike downloaded a template, for a letter. Homework was to write-and-save-and-print one, for Next Time. They made a start in the last few minutes of class.

'Make sure to underline your Heading,' Mike advised.

Ruby pecked away. <u>*Broken Dustbin*</u> stared back from the screen.

She'd phoned the Council twice, but her wonky wheelie-bin still sat lop-sided on the patio. Maybe they'll replace it if I write, she thought, awkward fingers jabbing at the keys.

Not certain what to say, she stared at _Broken Dustbin_ till her eyes watered, and the words fogged and blurred behind her pebble-specs.

Another heading drifted from the fog: _Freelance Fuel Engineer: Michael White_

Then the letter was on-screen no more, but clutched in her younger hand, and a gust of wind, not forecast, blew the *Ministry of Defence* envelope out of her frozen fingers into the shrubbery.

Michael was a straightforward husband, but a sought-after specialist when it came to fuel pumps. She never liked it when, in company, people asked him what he did. Why wouldn't he talk up his job a tiny bit? 'International fuel consultant' - or something impressive, but without sounding like Dorothy Clarke?

Not Michael. Straight out with it. 'Fuel pumps', he'd say.

Fuel pumps. As if a magic genie popped out when you rubbed one.

'Army, Navy, Air Force. When a fuel depot gets jammed up, they send for me,' he'd say. 'Anywhere in the world.'

It was Cyprus, in fact, and the RAF. The letter called it 'a refuelling incident'. They wouldn't say 'accident', for legal reasons. 'Accident' implies error and blame. But *in*cidents, oh, they happen all the time, and, by the way, your husband's dead.

'Saved money, did you, killing and cremating him in one?'

She'd said that to the woman from family liaison, swore

at her. *'You live in a different bloody world, you bloody people.'* Apologised, of course.

'We understand,' said Mrs Mullithorpe.

Mullithorpe? What sort of name is that?

'No, Mrs Mullithorpe! You don't understand! You can't! Unless they incinerated your husband too? In a bloody incident?'

Ruby wanted to apologise, for her rudeness, for her searing anger.

But in all the years since, she never had.

*

Mike was reminding them about homework.

'And please re-visit last week's learning, before next week.'

Last week.

Next week.

Will you come back, Ruby? Now you're a lass who's ace at cut-paste-save?

You never know, *Next Week*, through the miracle of computing you might Skype a conversation with the dead? Or cut-paste-save the speech Michael never made, at Janice and Graham's wedding? Cut and paste *Freelance Fuel Engineer: Michael White* into empty photographs, so Harry has a snap of mum and dad and Grandma, with a Grandpa too?

Ruby punched the 'off' button on the laptop, punched it hard, her pebble-glasses glaring at the spinning widget, a ridiculous toy train on a circular track, till it shunted itself into a dark tunnel. When she skewered the button next to the ink-well, the laptop slithered back into the depths.

She clawed her bag from the old wooden desk and was out the building before Dot Clarke could say a single snooty word about '*Next Week.*'

*

Ruby sat at the bulky desk-computer, hidden away in the dining room she no longer used. The screen could have been the mirror in the Ladies loo. When it lit up, her reflection disappeared.

Harry had downloaded her homework from the College link because she'd forgotten how, and the house was silent without him. She clicked on *Broken Dustbin* and her unfinished letter popped up.

Something to do. To pass the time.

Strange, though, to write a letter on a screen, pecking at plastic buttons that leave no mark. Fingers are for wrapping round a pen, flesh and blood guiding the ink, loops of letters bleeding from your heart onto white paper. Since the last letter to Michael, the one he never read, her flesh could hardly bear to touch a pen.

Now, pecking out dull words about wheelie-bins, she felt a welcome disconnect between slow fingers and hard plastic.

Fingertips on the keys below.

Words above, separate, behind a distant screen of glass.

Tapping.

Peering.

Tapping.

Peering.

No skin and flesh wrapping round a pen; no loops of letters bleeding from her heart; no smooth expectant page.

Ruby White: Machine.

She couldn't exactly say when her homework ceased to be a letter to the Council, or exactly why. But awkward hands grew fluent, and a fresh Heading appeared.

Michael White, Beloved

My loving Michael,

Ruby always called him that.

I've never not felt angry, ever since.

I've wanted to say why, but there's no-one I can tell, without you. I'm typing this into a machine, not by hand, because the old way, pen on paper, it's too…Can't find the word.

I won't promise to be quick, but we've time, the pair of us.

I was always happy when they sent you overseas - not for naughty reasons, you know that well enough. But doing what I wanted for a week or two, while knowing you were coming back, was…freshening? Like a secret liaison, waiting to happen. I told you this, in the last letter I wrote. I never imagined you not coming back. The only thing that came back was my letter. I still have it. And still read it. I'm still angry that you never did.

I called her Janice. Your mother's name. I'm angry you never saw her born, nor held her. Held us. I'm angry you never knew. It was in the letter that you didn't read. Janice has a youngster of her own now. Harry. And a husband, of course.

There was no-one else after you, Michael. Pigs sniffed at the sow but they didn't get fed.

I'm 73. I'm a Silver Surfer, learning computers and cut-paste-save. The teacher's name is Michael too, but we have to call him Mike. He's much younger than you were.

*

Ruby's fingers hurt.

It's not your fingers, Ruby.

She read the unfinished letter on the screen.

Ruby, it'll do. It's enough. And a long time coming.

She clicked on Save. Then Print.

With a kiss, the folded letter went into her special box, alongside her house deeds and the letter from the Ministry. And the one they returned, that Michael never saw.

Nor will you see this one, Michael. It's for me. Janice can read it, when the time comes. She'll show it to her husband, maybe get a grunt for her pains.

*

A new template opened on the screen, and Ruby tapped away at Broken Dustbin. Soon, the letter to the Council clattered from the printer too, and she tucked it in her homework file.

Getting quicker, Ruby White.

Ruby the Machine.

Preparing to switch off, she imagined a whirr, a shukk, and remembered Mike's advice: 'Be careful, and be tidy, when you use technology.' He never said 'computer'. That was Ruby's word. A right-click of the mouse and the menu popped up.

Through the window, she could see the garden bench, a gift from Janice. The old one rotted away. Some of the shrubs still flowered, older now.

Her mouse scrolled down to *Michael Stone Beloved.doc*

She didn't want young Harry chancing across her letter. Not yet.

In the strengthening wind, she thought she saw a flash of white, whisking up from the shrubbery into early evening sky. She imagined an envelope, but it was just dead leaves, waiting for autumn.

Ruby White, flesh and blood, clicked on 'Delete'.

Billy the Quid

Billy's the name. My pals, when I had some, used to call me Billy the Quid, because I'm careful with cash. Can't help it, brought up in the Fifties, when you earned what you could, and spent what you had, and not a quid or a penny more.

Folk these days, it's every bugger's money but their own.

Thanks to cancer, there's just me now. Too old to work, but all the same I work six days a week. Call me a lonely daft old git but I still run an old-style grocer's shop - old-fashioned, you'd call it, but it's mine. Three rooms and a loo, upstairs. Oh, and the van outside, about as old as I am.

I used to like it here, till online killed the other shops, and the arse-wipes moved in. No police on the streets to stop 'em anymore. Too stubborn to sell, me.

But then the robberies started.

Bloody *gun* in my face, can you believe it? We lost dad to *guns,* in World War Two, and for what? He was called Billy, as well. These scruffy drug-yobs now, they've guns or knives or both, and shaven heads like Nazis. I can still remember Brylcreem. And combs. And trying to look your best in a cut-price Burton's suit with side vents.

I'd ditch the shop tomorrow if anyone would buy it. I'd bugger off, somewhere or anywhere, sell up.

Well, I *think* I would.

Till then, I've *hardened* up instead. Had to. Shop's got a steel door now, window bars, CCTV, till-in-a-cage. My stock-room in the cellar, it's a fortress. When I was a kid you never even had to lock your door.

Can't keep them out though, thieves. It's when it's dark and the streets are empty and the till's full. That's when the cameras clock them, eyeing the booze, eyeing the day's takings. They've not popped in to buy pink plonk for Mother's Day, I can tell you that. Batty old Billy, easy money, that's what they think.

I might have grown old but I've not grown soft. First little tosser looked no more than twelve, all dolled up with tattoos and a flick knife. I broke his arm with a cricket bat, kicked his druggy arse into the gutter. When I say, 'he never knew what hit him', I mean I bet he'd never seen a cricket bat before.

Next, the crack-head arse-wipe who shoved the *gun* in my face. I'd 'taken measures' though. Hidden switch - click - and the steel door slams shut behind him. Jumpy thicko turns to look and I tazer the sod. You can get hold of anything you want these days - nice, nasty, it's all the same.

Down in the cellar, trussed up, he might've been a side of bacon - a piglet, more like. I could've kicked *his* arse back on the street too, I suppose. It was that gun, though, gun in my *face*, and after what guns did to dad? Old Billy the Quid's too long in the tooth for bleeding hearts, and not ashamed to say so.

I've got the van, you see, and the nights are dark, and it's only a mile down the road, is the land-fill site.

Jungle drums must've got the message out, because they started turning up in pairs, and after closing now. Two big buggers. Thing is, where electrics are concerned I don't lack brains. I'm handy, I was prepared.

'The old git's gonna wet hisself.'

I could hear them thinking it, when they tried to do the till. What 'the old git' did was trigger the special circuit. Pair of 'em went up like coffins in a crematorium. I lowered the voltage after, though, because of the smell. And I didn't want to burn the shop down, did I?

I'll be needing a bigger van.

Fifty years younger and I'd join the army, like dad. If I'm honest, when you're my age, shop-keeping's not all it's cracked up to be. Because as long as I keep earning, the arse-wipes round here'll keep stealing. They'll not stop. Every bugger's money but their own.

I won't sell up, though. Small folk like me, we have it tough, yes, but we're 'socially significant'. I read it, in the paper. And since I'm 'significant'...

You, you might call it a vocation. But Billy the Quid, he's just keeping the numbers down.

Till whenever.

A Bag for Life

Des parked his old bones on the wooden bench.

He knew the location of every bench between the shopping precinct and home. There were five in all, and this was Bench Four. When Wanda was alive, he never noticed them, because Wanda did the shopping - insisted on it. If she sent him, he bought the wrong things. Baked beans when she wanted green. Full-fat when she wanted semi-skimmed.

'Good job we don't need flour,' she'd say. 'You'd come back with a daffodil!'

These days, Des relied on the five benches. The older his legs became, the further away seemed the shops. He propped his 'bag for life' on the wooden slats and eased his aching muscles. Bench Four faced the old pond, stagnant now, and no ducks anymore. Foxes got them, probably. Or it might have been cats. Marauding cats. Or hooligans.

A young boy was swishing a heavy stick at the tall reeds fringing the pond, slicing their heads off, one after the other, excitement burning in his eyes. Seven, eight years old perhaps, and on his own. Des tutted. It was a Thursday. What happened to school? He should be learning.

The boy, as if telepathic, wandered over and said, 'my

mum's told me to wait here while she's at the shops because I slow her down.'

'Has she? No school today, then?'

'I'm to keep away from the pond and not talk to strangers.'

Well, Des said to himself, none out of two so far.

'What's in your bag, mister? Is it money?'

'Huh, fat chance.'

'Is it a bomb, then?'

This boy needs to be in school, thought Des.

'It's a bottle of milk, son. A paper. A loaf. And two cans of beans.'

'If you were my dad, it'd be cans of beer. That's all he's good for, my mum says.'

'Beers for pubs, son. It's tea at home.' Des smiled at the thought of tea. Only one more bench before the kettle boiled.

'She won't buy cans of beans no more. They make dad fart. When he farts, I join in, and she kicks us both outside. We've a football net, in our yard.'

'Does he let you win, eh, your dad?'

'No. He's rubbish. I just win.'

Des nodded. From the corner of his eye, he spotted a thin woman with two carrier bags tramping up the path towards the pond. He pulled his bag for life towards him for protection. He sensed what was coming.

The woman reached the bench, and stood, glowering at Des and the boy. Not a word was spoken. Words would happen 'at home'. Her bags went down, and the flat of her hand went up. At the sound of flesh slapping flesh, Des understood the heavy stick, the decapitated reeds. The boy fought back his tears but, like a trained monkey, hefted the carrier bags along the path after his mother. She glared at Des with poison in her eyes. When the boy caught up, she slapped him again.

Des looked away, at the stagnant pond, remembering the tall reeds and the cleanness of the water when he and Wanda were seven or eight. He gathered up his bag for life and headed for the final bench.

The second can of beans was a mistake. Two cans and a bottle made a heavy bag. From distance, he saw Bench Five was occupied, and his heart and legs sank. He hated asking strangers to 'budge up' so he could rest.

Pride.

Doesn't always sit well with age, he knew.

When his eyes focused on the seated figure, he recognised Sid Waller, from the bowls club. Heart and legs grew back. No budging up required, and a same-age voice to talk to - even if Sid muttered only drivel whenever he opened his mouth, and was given to wandering around town every day of the year, sun or snow, in aimless circles. Des flopped down, weary. Sid acted as if Des had been there since daybreak.

'I do agree, Des, it was the finest, the finest funeral. I do realise that, at the time, your mind's perhaps on other things, but all the same...'

Whether Sid meant Wanda's funeral, two years ago, or that of Sid's wife, three years before, Des had no idea. 'Yesterday' could be twelve hours or twelve years to Sid.

'Very kind, Sidney.'

'Did she make you buy that, Des? Your Wanda?' Sid tapped a finger on the bag for life that sat on the bench between them.

'You suggesting I chose it myself, Sid? With these fetching flowers printed on? No, it's Wanda's. I'd have something thick and brown, given the choice.'

'Get yourself one, then, Des. A thick, brown bag of your own.'

'Ah, but if this one breaks, Sid, they replace it. Free. It's a Bag for Life. That's why they call them that.'

'Have they, then?'

'Have they what?'

'Replaced it?'

'Oh, twice. First time when I left it on the patio and something ate through the corners. Ants maybe. Second time, I caught the handle on the gate and it snapped. The ants one, they quibbled. I said, stop calling it a Bag for Life then. They caved in. So, two new bags in two years. Both of them free.'

'Look after it, Des, your bag for life.'

'I must, Sid. It's Wanda's. We always go shopping together, pair of us.'

Both men fell silent. Des could think of nothing more to tell Sid Waller, and he was tiring of talk. Sid wandered off, without a word.

All five benches had sparked a conversation today. Not always the case when Des took his Bag for Life to the shops. While his legs recovered, he went through them.

Bench One, near the Newsagents: two women from the

Market, who'd budged up for him without being asked. He knew their faces, they his, so they'd passed the time of day for a good ten minutes. He couldn't recall anything they'd talked about.

Bench Two, next to the bakery: one of the drinkers who loitered there these days, till the wine shop opened or they got moved on. Usually both. Des got the man's life story - or a pack of dreams - but not his name. Used to be a jockey, professional, he claimed. Well, Des thought, you haven't half grown taller since.

Bench Three was between the shops and the old pond - the longest stretch. Des had the bench to himself till a young couple came along, and lit up. Neither Des nor Wanda ever smoked.

'Don' mind, mate, do you?'

Yes, I do. It'll make my clothes stink. 'No, no. You're alright.'

Smoke blew in his face. When the couple began canoodling, he said his good mornings and loped to Bench Four, despite his legs.

Des glossed over the reed-snapping boy and his angry mother at the stagnant pond, remembering instead the way Bench Four used to be.

Ducks. Cleanness. Reeds.

Wanda.

Bench Five, the nearest to home, was Sid Waller, whose bowed back was growing smaller as he wandered off to nowhere. Sid was a long-time widower, but seemed only half-certain of the fact. Des didn't know what to make of him.

Should 'home' be called *Bench Six*?

No. Benches were ports in a storm. Home was your harbour. He could drop anchor at home, unpack his shopping, and put the kettle on. Carefully, he lifted his Bag for Life and shuffled off.

It began to rain as his key turned in the front door, and rain rattled the windows as the kettle boiled. Wanda's Bag for Life sat safely on the kitchen table. When darkness fell, Des would read the paper, with beans on toast, and tea with fresh milk.

His lunchtime tea was different altogether. He placed two cups and two saucers on a tray, with a milk jug and the warmed pot. With conscious pleasure, he poured boiling water over proper leaf tea and carried the tray next door. Returning for the almost empty Bag for Life, he placed it reverentially by the tea things.

'We remembered to buy semi-skimmed this time, eh, Wanda? It's just as you like it,' he said, pouring tea into two china cups, and removing from the Bag for Life a small silver box. Two years ago, he'd filled the box with the very greatest care and, in his man-shed, soldered it permanently closed.

'Don't let your tea go cold, Wanda.'

He drank his, and put the empty cup and saucer back on the tray.

'We had a fine old walk, eh?' he told the silver box. 'Folk at every bench today. Youngsters, market people, Sid Waller. Even a jockey. Had a good natter with all of them, didn't we, the pair of us?'

With tenderness, he replaced the silver box on the special shelf by the window, next to the urn containing the rest of Wanda's ashes.

'Yes, a fine walk,' he said, reaching for the second cup.

He raised it to Wanda, in remembrance, and drank her tea.

Mrs Melanie

Monday

I don't know her name, the woman on the bus. If she's told me, I've forgotten. I'm hopeless with names. She doesn't know I'm Vivienne - Viv, that is. Because I've never said.

We talk, regardless, if a double seat's free. To and from, ever since I started at the Chemist's. If there's no seats, she pretends she's pregnant. It's just puppy-fat, but two ticks later she's off her pins.

I'd try it myself, when the bus is packed. But age is against me.

I say to her, gone six-o-clock and not home yet. Supposed to finish at five but TFC said we'd cocked up the stock-take. He was right, we had, but he might've...oh, whatever. When I say TFC, she knows I mean The Fat Controller. On a pig-rotten day I abbreviate him to Bastard. If I didn't, I'd have to admit being Whingey Cow, and who's going to do that?

She has a giggle. She understands.

I remind her his real name's Pat McKnoller. He's no fatter than she is, but I don't say the last bit out loud.

Who's 'we'? she asks. Who'd cocked up the stock-take?

'We', I tell her, is me and Mary-Anne. It's a doll's name, isn't it? Except she's 56 - two years younger than me. I don't tell her that. Mary-Anne's only holiday cover and stock-takes so we don't much coincide. We managed tea and a hot panini once, in Cafe Nero.

I don't much coincide with anyone.

She's had a rotten day, the woman on the bus, in a warehouse. She's a packer and it ruins her hands. It's feet with me, I say, on rotten days. Standing up, dawn to dusk, The Fat Controller's flickering eyeballs watching you, one tough customer after another. Barely time to bite on a crispbread or pop your bottom on a loo.

By 'tough customer', I don't mean they'd punch us. It's not A&E on a Saturday night. We're a Chemist shop. Truth be told, our lot are too polite for my taste. Wait their turn, say please - even smile. Days'd pass quicker if they had a bit of umph.

No. What's tough is...having to see them.

Red-rashed kids, and you think, is it Meningitis? Folk queuing for prescriptions and you know it's either diabetes or after-cancer-pills. And that tap-tap-tap of sticks when the old ones totter in. They're the toughest.

Snails.

Dragging out the pain.

I worked in a department store, way back, before it went tits up. I was Perfume/Cosmetics. A much younger crowd. In they'd flit, for a Make-up demo or a Facial.

'Will this take ten years off? Like it says in the leaflet?'

'Ooh, course it will!'

The Fib Counter, I used to call it. But not to the customers. Or the boss.

Mr McKnoller, The Fat Controller, he wouldn't have stood for it. Customer begins with a capital 'C', and 'C' is for Care, he says. 'Care is what we do'. He drills it in. Under my breath, I tell him 'C' stands for Cash, because I need a roof over my head and they don't come free.

Thursday

I'm telling the woman on the bus about this old biddy, who practically lives in the shop. Ancient, one of the snails. Me, itching to leave. Her, glad to arrive.

'Name?' I ask her. No, I don't. I'm Polite, Patient, Precise. We learnt the three P's in staff training. Drilled into us, by TFC.

'Could I have your name, please?' I say.

'Melanie', she says. Customers get away with just one word, don't they? I want to say, 'Melanie what?' but I come out with, 'I beg your pardon. I meant your surname.'

I do *surname* in what The Fat Controller calls 'a rising inflection'. Polite.

'Melanie', she repeats, with that sharp look customers give you. Me, Polite and Patient go AWOL, and I fall back on plain-old Precise.

'Melanie's not your first name, then?'

'It's Mrs Melanie', she says. '*Mrs* Melanie.' 'I'm in Mr McKnoller's medicine book.'

I'm not allowed near The Fat Controller's medicine book. I grovel over and ask him.

'That's correct. It's *Mrs* Melanie,' he says. 'Interesting surname.' And he reaches across to Prescriptions and puts his chubby hand on a paper package. Without having to look, it seems to me.

'She's a regular', he says. He hands me the package and goes back to mixing potions.

I read the wrapper. There's seven different pills and a cream, and she gets a new lot once a month. Knows when she's running out because the rattling stops, poor soul.

The woman on the bus has a giggle at this.

I hand over the pills, but Mrs Melanie sits down in 'the chair', tears open the pack - which takes forever - and checks each one. She's Patient and Precise, I'll give her that. But it's not Polite, is it? Implying we make mistakes. Well, that *I* do, since I'm Johnny-on-the-spot.

But there's more. Following day, she's in again, with the wrapper with the list on. What TFC calls 'the chair', is tucked to the side of the counter. 'For the aged, the infirm, or the bored,' he once explained. She lowers herself into it, not that there's much to lower, parks her stick, and asks for Mr McKnoller.

I want to snap, 'He's *OUT*, so you're lumbered with me!'

'I'm afraid he's unavailable at present', I snivel.

'Mmph', she says. Told you, customers get away with just one word. Then no words at all, just silence. Her one good eye runs down the list, up again, down again, up again. She could be at Bingo.

'May I be of any assistance, meanwhile?' I do, I say 'meanwhile'.

‘My cream’, she says. Her stick pushes at the floor, and she rises from ‘the chair’ like a wraith, gripping my arm with bony fingers. She drops her plummy voice as if a State Secret’s on the way. Shop’s empty, but she drops her voice. ‘*Mr* Melanie says an unusually tiny tube has been supplied,’ she whispers. ‘Which may not last.’

Her watery eye fixes me. The other’s buried under wrinkles and a saggy lid. ‘Please record our disquiet, and advise Mr McKnoller, on his return,’ she tells me, with a glance at ‘the chair’. Then she remembers sitting in it for a good ten minutes, not thirty seconds ago, so she shuffles away on her stick.

I get a flickery eyeball from Mr McKnoller when I pass on the message.

‘Yes. She does that’, is all he says.

Wednesday

They’ve got new overalls, at the warehouse, and the woman on the bus is showing hers off. It’s sort of brown-green, like dysentery, but it’s comfy, and doesn’t rub, she says. I remind her we wear only white at the Chemist’s. We’re *medical*, I explain.

She wants the next instalment of Mrs Melanie and I almost say, ‘we’re a Chemist not a TV soap.’ But to pass the time, I tell her.

Mrs M, she totters through the door and drops straight into ‘the chair’, breathless. I’m thinking we should screw a little clip to the side, for walking sticks. Hers clatters down, soon as she parks it, and she can't bend, so it's muggins has to come out from behind and pick it up. But she does mumble thank you.

I roll out my staff training, 'Anything I can help you with, Mrs Melanie?' I get a smile for remembering her name.

'I'm here on behalf of *Mr* Melanie…I came in for his…for his…' She stops, blank, and I do too. We're two snails in a photo. Then the shutter freezes altogether and time stops. I look over my shoulder at Mr McKnoller, top of his eyes anyway, sticking up above Prescriptions. He just shakes his visible bits and carries on. By the time I look back at Mrs M, she's thawed herself out, pushed herself up on her stick and is wandering towards the door.

'We appreciate your assistance', she says, not that I've done a thing for either of them, and leaves.

She's in six times a week, one excuse or another, something for her, something for him, till her pill-supply runs out. Then, end of the month, we start again. If it's not the cream that's wrong, and it never is, it's too-few-pills.

'She does take the pills,' Mr McKnoller assures me. 'Must. To live. Doubtless the odd one disappears behind the fridge. Easily done, as age sets in…' Then he stops too, frozen, like Mrs M, and I'm reminded TFC's no duckling either.

Next second, he's shovelling pills for others to swallow. Me, I'm the go-between-piggy-in-the-middle. At least neither him nor Mrs M pretend they're young. A customer came back when I was at Perfumes/Cosmetics, sixty-something and a few besides, complaining I sold her a lipstick that nobody wants to kiss.

She giggles again, the woman on the bus.

We both do.

Friday

Just me on the bus tonight.

Three months I've been at the Chemist's, and it's never gone away, that tightening on my skin, when the old ones totter through. If I got a pound every time I lowered an oldie into 'the chair'... And winched one out again.

The woman I used to talk to, she's disappeared. I wish I'd told her I'm a Vivienne, even though she seemed more of a Shaz. They've changed the bus routes, you see - for 'efficiency', the local paper said. My journey's twice as long, and if I'm honest I'm too pooped for gossip, from or to. If she *was* sitting here, I'd not be saying 'Fat Controller' anymore. It's Mr Mac, my new nickname for the boss. I've warmed to him, despite the longer days.

It's two slow buses now, then near enough a mile walk from bus to home. I slam the front door closed and shoot the bolt, kick my shoes along the carpet and lean against the wall. If I flopped into the hall chair I'd struggle to get out again. Can't say I've ever danced down my hallway to the kitchen, but never have I tottered down as tortoise-like as this.

I'll be needing a stick, at this rate. I'm becoming a shuffler. Might have to screw a little clip to the hall chair.

Tuesday

Bank Holiday weekend we were closed, and the Monday. A nice break to…well, I cleaned the patio, because it's never used and collects all sorts. And back-to-back films on TV, black and white, with Fred Astaire.

Come Tuesday, I'm glad to be at work, busy though we are. I'm finishing up when I see the white packet in Prescriptions. Should've been collected days ago but folk go on holiday and don't tell *us*. The uncollected packs go in a 'Late' box, for double-checking. I'm closing the lid when I spot 'Mrs Melanie' on the label. Been so discombobulated these last few days, I never noticed she'd not been in. You know, for her rituals.

I go backstage - that's what I call Prescriptions now - and tell Mr Mac.

'Oh. Yes.'

That's all he says. He reaches for the Medicine Book. I don't know why we call it that. It's just a printout of stuff on the PC screen. He takes a ruler and runs it down the page till it reaches 'M', and with a black pencil he draws two long lines through 'Mrs Melanie'. A few tapped keys and the PC stutters out spaces where her name once was. He nods at Mrs Melanie's prescription.

'Please put that in Waste', he says. Once a prescription's been issued, there's no sending it back.

'Poor Mrs Melanie', I say. I don't know what else *to* say. 'And poor *Mr* Melanie, now.'

Mr Mac does one of his long pauses. 'There is no Mr Melanie'.

I suppose I knew she was a widow, poor soul. Always in the shop alone. And wouldn't any Mr Melanie worth his salt have collected her prescription for her?

Mr Mac pushes out his lips. 'There never was a Mr Melanie,' he adds. 'She never married.'

He freezes into a photo. I could go deaf, from the clock ticking.

'So, she was *Miss* Melanie?' I pluck up courage to ask.

His eyeballs do that little flicker thing. Still not sure what it means. Then, silence.

I reach for my coat, but Mr Mac begins to talk. Sort of to himself.

A bit like me and the woman on the bus.

'We called her Miss Melanie, in class. Melanie Brooke was her real name. She was my teacher. Primary School. She taught me to read. And had a lovely reading voice herself. 'Please Miss Melanie, read us a story', we'd say. She was going to anyway, but taught us to ask politely. She made words special. She was always Miss Melanie, to us and everyone else, and the name stuck, I suppose. She gave her life to that school.'

My feet are so tired I almost sit down in 'the chair'. He doesn't like us using it when there's customers, but we're closed now. In any case, for Mr Mac it could have been midnight on a Sunday.

'After I'd qualified, I passed the School every day, driving into town to my very first job, as a young chemist. And the staff room window overlooks the road. It's next to the traffic lights, so I'd often have to wait. When I was on earlies, so was she. In the window, on her own, working. When I was on lates, the same. Never a Mr Melanie to make breakfast for in the morning, or dinner at night. She was her work, and that was that.'

Mr Mac raises his head, and looks round, at his own work, at Prescriptions, at 'the chair', at the door where eyes shuffle in and shoulders shuffle out. At the Medicine Book, with its black lines pencilled through a name.

'Not a widow, then?'

'No. Never married.' He looks at the PC, with its deletions. 'Not everyone does.'

I want to say something. About him. But I can't.

I fall back on *her,* instead.

'But, *Mrs* Melanie?'

'Yes. That began when she retired - ill health. I can't imagine her leaving the School voluntarily. She doddered in here one morning. I'd only bought the shop a day or two before.'

'Why, Miss Melanie', I said. 'How lovely to see you.' I expected her to say, 'Goodness, it's little Patrick McKnoller', and test me on my nine times tables. She didn't even know me.'

"*Miss* Melanie? How *dare* you?' she said. She was cross. Perhaps not with me. I don't know who or what she was cross with.'

"I'll have you know I am *Mrs* Melanie. Address me as such, or have *Mr* Melanie to contend with!' The voice was still there. Rich. Silken vowels. I wanted her to read me a story. But I could only gape.'

"'Of course,' I said to her. 'I do apologise, *Mrs* Melanie. How may I help?'

Polite. Patient. Precise.

"'My prescription. There.' She pointed to the shelves behind. 'Mr Farringdon always has it ready. Ordinarily, I do not need to ask.'

Mr Mac half-smiles, his eyes still doing that flickery thing.

'She was unaware Mr Farringdon no longer owned the shop. Nor that he was...no longer. I continued doing for her what he had done. If the School supplied her previous needs, it was the Pharmacy supplying them now.'

I remember Mr Mac, at staff training. 'C is for Care,' he'd say. 'We're much more than pills, creams and potions.'

Then he starts talking again, sort of to himself, sort of to me.

'As her illness worsened, the ritual visits grew more bizarre. Four, five, six times a week, month on month. We - I - took them as seriously as her physical ailments, because...because what can be prescribed for loneliness?'

I don't imagine he's really asking *me*, so I just shrug.

'Beyond her work, Miss Melanie struggled - struggled to *be* somebody, I suppose. Out of her struggle came *Mrs* Melanie, and into my Medicine Book Mrs Melanie went. She invented her 'husband' to complete the cure.' His eyes flicker again. 'Such as it was.'

Mr Mac's voice is growing quieter now, and I figure it's time I left him in peace. I back towards the door, but wouldn't you know it, I bump into 'the chair'.

'Do you know, Vivienne, it was me who bought that chair? Entirely to ease Mrs Melanie's ritual visits. I'm not one for rituals, myself. I'm not a churchgoer, or a bon viveur. I'm not a joiner of clubs. But Mrs and Mr Melanie were as real as you or me. Who was I to put an end to them?'

I slip on my coat in the silence, and sort of sneak out. Mr Mac, he's working up to tears.

I missed my bus.

I knew I would.

Wednesday

Nobody to talk to on the bus this morning, and the traffic awful.

Same last night. Took an age to get home. When I did, my shoes went tumbling down the hallway. I kicked one off, kicked the other after it, and if I'd had three legs I'd have kicked the third so hard it would've smashed through the back door and splattered across the patio I never use.

I had to sit down in the hall chair. I sat for an age, with two chops going off in the fridge. Haven't the nerve to ask the butcher for one, though one's plenty. They went uncooked last night, the chops.

I was thinking of Mr Mac, shedding a tear for Mrs Melanie. I shed a tear for her too.

Then before I know it, I'm shedding tears for him as well. *Dammit,* I thought, we should be shedding tears for

Mrs Melanie together. He might've been there all night for all I know, all alone, flickering his eyeballs in Prescriptions. I was too Polite, too Patient with him.

The third 'P', it shouldn't stand for 'Precise'. It bloody-well ought to be for *Personal.*

But all I managed was a lollop on my old backside, shoes kicked along the carpet, two raw chops in the fridge.

I sat, scraping my fingernails on the arms of the chair, salt tears on my cheeks for Mrs and Mr Melanie. And for Mr Mac.

And for me.

I suppose.

And the Next Train Is…

Ben's last exam was a bitch. But it *was* the last.

The final-final, ha-ha.

Now, the *what-next* clock was ticking, fast and loud. Where could an un-travelled student go with an almost-degree in Sociology?

Offers so far, nil.

Home to Axminster first, to swap crumpled revision notes for a cold can of lager. He thrust the dog-eared pile into his retro messenger bag, and twiddled his phone, like worry beads. The sound of trains juddering past his grubby bedroom window would help postpone *what-next* for another day.

Ben liked trains.

But not railway platforms. The 12.41 was already ten minutes late. His phone battery had died from over-use, and opportunities for people-watching consisted of two wrinklies squatting on a scratched metal bench by the unmanned ticket office.

Not 'unmanned', Ben. Un*staffed*. Gender parity. Call yourself a Sociologist?

The first woman was dressed for shopping, with flat shoes and an empty bag. The older woman wore light walking boots and a waterproof, a small backpack beside her. Despite his political correctness, 'a pair of old crones' flashed into Ben's head. He looked around, hoping for more interesting bodies to watch, but none arrived.

The train did, finally. He flopped onto a double-seat, tempted to slap his trainers on the upholstery, despite the warning sign. The carriage was empty, his own private train.

Peace.

As the carriage door shucked open, the older woman from the bench tottered past lines of empty seats towards him. She'll be heading for the 'Quiet' carriage next door, he predicted. The old ones usually do.

She sat down.

Right next to him.

Her backpack flopped onto the opposite seat.

There's fifty empty places! he wanted to scream. *Go somewhere else, you wizened hag!*

To Ben's horror, she began to talk, *uninvited*, in a voice somewhere between Old Crone and Duchess.

'Are you travelling alone?' she said.

He stared at her, at the blank seats around them, and, hammy perhaps, craned his neck to stare at each end of the empty carriage.

'I do beg your pardon. It wasn't a question to you. I was remembering, aloud, my previous conversation with the lady on the platform there.' She waved a grey hand at the woman with the shopping bag, who waved back as the train shunted forward and picked up speed.

'Her name is Anthea, I learned, and she's waiting for the Plymouth train. The opposite direction to me. And to you, of course. Anthea was asking, are you travelling alone? Why not? I replied. I always do.'

Me too - given the choice!

'A strange question, don't you think? I mean, I *sleep* alone. Occasionally, with regret. Frequently, in blissful peace. Any snoring is mine, and thus acceptable.'

Ben wondered why an almost-degree in Sociology hadn't prepared him for this.

'Twice a week, I visit a railway station. I have both bus pass and Senior Citizens Railcard. *Have cards, will travel.*'

She treated Ben to a chuckle that sounded like a drain being cleared.

'At the station, I peruse the board - where the trains are…advertised? Displayed? No matter. I wait for the names of stations to appear, and I read them. When I like the sound of a name, I buy a ticket. And I go there.' She chuckled again. 'Alone.'

I wish you were, thought Ben. He considered plugging himself into his earphones, but inbuilt decency stopped him. And a dead battery.

'Sometimes, I alight at a mere village. With perhaps a single street, a single shop. I enter, browse, converse. Always. I buy a card or something small, a memento. Exploring is all very well, but one must remember where one's been?'

A brief pause. Ben figured no response was required.

'There may be a café or a pub. For lunch. If not, my

trusty knapsack contains provisions.' She patted it, with a hand made entirely of knuckles. 'I enjoy the combination, you see?'

This pause was longer, a response expected.

'Combination? Of what?'

'Why, of spontaneity, and preparation. Isn't that the secret of life?'

'Is it?'

She lowered her voice, in the empty carriage. 'They don't let you know the secret till you're older. When life has squeezed the spontaneity out of you. Be prepared to put it back, young man. Or die.'

Guilt pierced him. Why mention dying? Was she ill? He glanced at her furrowed skin and bony frame. She looked...old. The way an old, normal person is supposed to look. Likes babbling on, he thought. Well, Sociology's a Social Science, Ben. Be Social, at least. Just don't expect much Science.

'So, which 'mere village' will you 'alight' at today?'

'Today? Whimple. Such an interesting name. Isn't a whimple something worn by a nun? If so, why name a village after it - or a railway station? I shall discover. It's neither terribly large nor terribly far. A shop, a pub, a church - the spine of every English village. And people in the street, of course, to ask.'

'Ask them what Whimple means?'

'Ask anything and everything. *Asking* is the key. Ask ten people to extoll their village, and ten different answers come your way - all of interest. But I begin by asking for directions. Then converse. People do, given the chance.' She glanced at Ben, with a slight smile. 'And one must talk not merely with the old, but with the young. Always.'

My lucky day. 'The young? Why?'

She unfolded five wrinkled fingers at him, upturned. 'We are doing the 'why', surely? Here and now?'

Ben's look was pure puzzlement.

'How to explicate?' she said.

He wanted to add, 'don't bother', but she was off again.

'Because of generational differences? In language, for example? In personal history? My personal history is rather more advanced than yours - I suspect you have noticed?'

Ben tried to pretend he hadn't, but her drain-clearing chuckle put a stop to that.

'And sharing such history may fascinate the young. Or be a bore.'

She took in Ben's red trainers, tattooed wrist, and messenger bag, a crumpled pack of revision notes poking out of it.

'Particularly while their own history is still in the making?'

What is she talking about? thought Ben.

'My journey today, alas, is too brief for shared histories. Even were it not, mine may be alien to you. Yours to me, likewise. This is our very first meeting, after all. But I still seek to know. To imagine. I've already imagined you, a tiny bit, through your dress, your posture.'

Ben tried not to sit up straight, but sit up straight he did.

'Too often, personal histories are mere internal monologues, no? But one's personal history ought to be a set of *conversations.* So, I'm also imagining you through what you say.'

Say? I've hardly got a word in!

'Doubtless you are doing the same with me?'

Though too polite to admit it, yes, when she shed her waterproof, Ben had scanned her closely. Expensive clothing, but hardly new. Quality material, well-cut. Mended at the sleeves now, but with care. Clean, crisply ironed. No wedding ring. Wristwatch *probably* gold. Coiffed grey locks, not long out of the salon. Upright posture. And her language inescapably of the 'elaborated code'. He'd done Social Observation, in Year Two.

Nevertheless, he clumsily changed the subject. 'How long will you give it? In Whimple, I mean?'

She noted the shift.

'It depends,' she said, 'on the response of those I meet.'

She said it in a neutral tone, but his guilt level soared.

'I have yet to encounter a ghost town. Dog walkers generally pass the time of day. One asks. They tell. We converse. Occasionally, I will knock on a friendly-looking door and request a glass of water. Whoever answers can see immediately I mean no harm. You would agree, I imagine?'

Ben gave her a smile-shrug. 'Harmless, maybe,' he almost said. 'But not speechless!'

The train read his mind. It slowed, and a disembodied voice announced, 'the next station is *Whimple, Whimple.*'

She took her backpack and rose from the seat. 'I do hope I haven't imposed?' she said.

‘Er, no, of course not,’ he lied, as the train sidled up to the tiny station.

‘It’s as I was telling the lady on the platform.’ She flipped five ancient knuckles at the distance. ‘I venture out alone. But never back alone. Without fail, I encounter fellow members of the human race, and return with the experience.’

Ben’s guilt quotient rocketed now. Had he shaped up as a fellow member of the human race? What ‘experience’ of him would she be taking back?

She smiled. ‘It’s the going there, and asking,’ she said. ‘That’s the key. One. Must. Ask.’

She smiled again, and was gone. Within seconds, Whimple also disappeared.

Ben’s red trainers flopped onto a now-empty seat, in an act of petty defiance. He leaned back and wallowed in the silence. Not far to Axminster, where a cold lager and a laptop waited.

And the future.

Unknown.

What did Old Lady Crone say? Something about his personal history still being in the making? *Interfering old bag.*

He glared through the stained window at flickers of landscape, as the train’s dull throb joined the pulse of the rails.

Tocketa-tocketa. Tocketa-tocketa.

A nagging backbeat of rising guilt added a rhythm of its own, before the *what-next* clock joined in.

Ticketa-ticketa. Ticketa-ticketa.

Ben tried to shape his thoughts, but they dripped and slipped beneath the juddering wheels of the train.

Ticketa-ticketa.

Tocketa-tocketa.

Axminster was suddenly there, the station signs laddering past the window, then familiar sounds of brakes and carriage doors and trundled luggage. A disembodied voice said, 'this is Axminster, Axminster. The next station is Crewkerne…'

Ben lifted his red trainers off the seat.

And put them back again.

He was no longer in the right frame of mind for a grubby-windowed room overlooking the railway.

Three years of hard graft, and the day I polish off my Sociology finals, what's my reward? Some old crone plonks herself down uninvited on the next seat - in an empty carriage - and shoves a Sociology lecture down my throat!

By the time he'd glugged the best part of a bottle of water to cool himself, the train had chugged out of Axminster.

Tocketa-tocketa.

With him still on it.

The alien view from the window was a gravelly river whose name he didn't know, winding its way past anonymous villages in the far distance. He'd never been to Crewkerne, didn't even like the name. His habits were to the west, and Crewkerne was east, a few miles up the line.

Barely sat down and I'm making polite noises while Lady Crone rambles on - and loads me with guilt, on top of wrestling with what-next. No wonder I'm postponing. Why else would I suddenly decide to go to Crewkerne?

Which is what he seemed to be doing.

Ticketa-ticketa.

Tick.

He stepped down onto a deserted platform.

Crewkerne station was *unstaffed*, and the waiting room and loos firmly locked. Within seconds, he wished he'd got off at Axminster. Outside, what faced him was a car park, a builders' merchant, a housing estate, and a café - closed. He walked to the main road, and spotted a pub some distance away.

Too early for pubs. And no more aimless chatter with strangers, *please*.

Trudging further, he realised the town itself was a walloping hike in the distance. He took stock. Crewkerne might be a fascinating place, but he measured the return slog too, and decided against it.

Back on the platform, the digital display rolled forward, reminding him the next Axminster train was almost an hour away. So much for spontaneity, Ben. He flopped down on a bench. Alone. A free newspaper lay discarded on the seat, and for something to do, he flicked through it.

A feature on pig-farming.

Arson at a local scout-hut.

What-to-do this week in your garden. Ben didn't have a garden.

The jobs page - tiny wages for working in a petrol station, a coffee-shop, a burger bar.

No thanks!

About to put the paper down, he spotted a smallish ad, with a heading in bold - 'Suit Young Graduate', it said. The pay was modest. 'Management Trainee Opportunity', above the details of a local Housing Trust. His mood lifted, guilt quotient dipping back almost to normal. His Year Three dissertation was on social housing. He believed in it.

With a passion.

The Trust had a Crewkerne address. Ben had no idea what Crewkerne was like, for work or for play, but he automatically reached for his phone.

Dead.

In the deserted station, he blew out his breath and stared at the number, street name, and postcode, before throwing the newspaper back on the seat. He could always write to them. Maybe tomorrow?

Yes.

Tomorrow.

Ben checked the newspaper's date.

Today.

A voice not quite his own said, 'Or you could capitalise on chance, Ben? You studied social metaphor in Year One, remember? Why not bite the bullet, grasp the nettle, and strike while the iron is hot?'

Or just go there. You've bothered to travel. Why return empty-handed?

A female voice in his skull now, the rattle of an old crone, triggered a wry smile of recognition.

'It's the going there, and asking. That's the key. One. Must. Ask.'

He got to his feet, uncertain red trainers tapping on the flagstones. Then he made up his mind - something of a departure, for him.

'Get your legs into Crewkerne,' his own voice said. 'And ask for directions.'

Yes. Ask a stranger.

Ben's dead phone - and the newspaper - slid into his messenger bag. With personal history in mind, he strode from an empty railway station onto the unknown streets of *what-next.*

42nd Street

The Beetlecrushers clog-dancing team clicked and tapped their way across South Petherton village square. Folk Festival Day was warm and muggy - shirtsleeves and pushchairs, panting dogs, the smell of fried onions, fresh pizza and spit-roast Dexter beef, wafting from West Street and the courtyard of The Brewers Arms.

A fiddler bowed a single note and the crowd, squatting on lines of straw bales, stilled to a murmur. Two guitars mirrored the note. A bearded mandolin player fine-tuned his strings as eight rainbow-coloured dancers slid fresh flower-stems into hats of yellow straw.

Leaning on his stick, an old man shuffled towards the one remaining bale, helping his frail companion ease slowly down. It wasn't comfy, the bale, but at least it was a seat.

'Hope I can get up again', she said.

'I'll give y'a push.'

'Tuh, you couldn't push a fly, these days.'

He looked at his gnarled hands. No, he thought, these days the fly would win.

'Keep still', she said. 'They're goin' to start.'

The pair of them watched as bright skirts swished to the music, and felt the first beat as eight clogs rose and hovered over the ground, pausing for muscle-tearing moments before dropping to the tarmac with a single *click*. Eight more beats and eight more again, the rhythm quickening to the trill and ching of mandolin and guitars, and the fiddle spinning tight circles of sound which the tapping dancers chased and caught.

'You're tapping your stick', she whispered, pointing. He was following the beat, hadn't noticed.

'Well, *you're* tapping your foot. I saw you.'

'Tuh, tapping the good one,' she said, rubbing at the bandage on the other.

Skirts swirled and spun as the dance grew faster, his well-worn stick and her one good foot involuntarily tapping, tapping to the circles of sound, to the rhythm of clogs, tapping the two of them back, tapping their memories back, back to 1934 in Yeovil, to The Gaumont Cinema on Stars Lane, where they 'stepped out' together for the very first time, his arm around her warm young shoulders in the back row of the celluloid palace, watching Dick Powell's dancers in *42nd Street*, and she asking him, 'who's best, Ginger Rogers or Ruby Keeler?'

And him saying, 'You are.'

As one, the dancers climbed into the air on invisible strings, landing and spinning, eight clogs tapping and heeling, tapping and heeling, before the music flicked to a sudden stop - *click!* - and eight pointed toes slow-slow-slowly rose, knee-high, the audience rising with them, breath held, tensing, waiting, for one final rhythmic *clack!* Then eight toes falling in teasing-lingering-unison till they touched the ground with the tiniest of clicks, and the smiling dancers bowed.

Whoops and whistles rattled the windows of the homes and shops surrounding the square as applause swelled and fell, its last echoes fading into silence somewhere between the Delicatessen and the Pharmacy.

Then the crowd dispersed and the tapping dancers were gone, pitching the two companions out of their cinema seats, out of The Gaumont, spinning them back from 1934 to a new century, all the way back to an old straw bale in the emptying village square.

'I wish I could dance like that,' she sighed.

'You are', he said, his stick pointing at her one good foot, still tapping.

A Spot of Grease on the Microwave

Miriam jerked her head away, but the invisible string yanked it back again.

Miriam, this must stop! she said to herself. You have people waiting!

The string couldn't care less. It yanked, and forced her to stare, once more, at the same pointless silly thing. Was it *really* what she thought? Or was it her bloody eyesight?

Don't swear, Miriam, even if just in your head! It's a waste of thoughts!

Thoughts were hardly piling up, jamming the traffic, tooting their horns, shouting "think me!'

'Perhaps it is your bloody eyesight, after all!'

Did she say it out loud? She listened at the kitchen door. No. They didn't hear. With the tail of her Tuesday cardigan, she gave her thick spectacles a sharp rub and clamped them back on her nose: same cottagey kitchen; same amateur paintings on the wall - 'on the naive side of naive, deahr, don't you think?' That was Elspeth's view.

She ran the tap and washed Elspeth down the Belfast sink. Stained and chipped, like you, Miriam. Through the window, she scanned each tidy plant in - Elspeth again - 'that gaudy little gorden of yours.'

No, it wasn't her eyesight.

The invisible string jerked, her head turned, and, yes, the damn thing was still there - smeared on the microwave, in her tiny kitchen, on a Tuesday, in daylight.

Mesmerised, she stared.

Miriam could have been on the moon.

With a chattery '*tuhuhuh*' that passed for laughter, Bernette's tweet of a voice brought Miriam down to earth again, an earth suddenly full - that was exactly the word, *full* - of the two 'friends' for whom she ought to be making afternoon tea. Next door in Miriam's lounge ['one doesn't say *lounge* these days, deahr,' warned Elspeth], budgerigar-Bernette twittered at something Elspeth said.

Or at nothing at all.

Since the budgie's post-retirement move to what Elspeth called 'our jewelled village', Bernette had jabbered a true-blue Britisher song, despite her foreign-sounding name. Miriam was bemused. Why not enjoy being unusual? Why not luxuriate?

Plain old Miriam, who'd give her Tuesday cardigan and her spectacles to have been christened Bernette.

*

In the tiny kitchen, the string yanked once more and Miriam stared. That spot of grease was still there on the microwave. A bad buy, harsh white enamel showing every splash and smear.

She wanted to buy the apple-green one, but Elspeth said green was 'too bold a colour for constricted kitchens', the cow. And this morning, of all mornings, Miriam had managed to miss that spot of grease.

Tuesday mornings she carbolically cleaned her tiny house, because Tuesday afternoon was her turn to do tea for the three of them – and 'tea' meant covert inspection by sanitary inspectors masquerading as 'friends'.

They took tea, the three of them, on Tuesdays, Wednesdays and Thursdays, 'to break up the week with some company'. Elspeth's career as a secretary - 'an *admenestrator*, Miriam, it's entirely defferent!' - had helped her concoct the scheme.

Fridays, Elspeth reasoned, were for planning the weekend's agenda.

Mondays were for acting on matters arising.

The weekend itself meant shopping, events, and Any Other Business.

Only midweek needed 'breaking up'. And what better way than afternoon tea on a rota basis in their three different dwellings? For Bernette, the chance to tweet in a fresh cage was only too welcome. Even Miriam, amazed at being included, had 'nothing better to do'.

So, the rota began: Miriam, Tuesday; Bernette, Wednesday; tea with Elspeth on Thursday.

'Oh, look! The Queen's Honours List!' Bernette had chirped.

The others stared in confusion.

'*M*iriam, *B*ernette, *E*lspeth! Don't you see?'

They didn't.

'Our initials! M.B.E! We're an MBE! Tuhuhuh!'

Bernette cawed at her little insight. Elspeth laughed her dry laugh, *huck*, disguising a private fantasy in which she thanked the Queen for the medal she had long-deserved, perhaps for services to Snobbery.

'*M*ajor *B*loody *E*rror', Miriam predicted, to herself.

*

She peeked round the kitchen door, but her tea-companions were heads-together, preoccupied.

Elspeth was basking in Bernette's supposed 'je ne sais quoi'.

'*Huh. Je ne sais quaaark!*' thought Miriam.

Hoping mystique-dust might rub off, Elspeth had brokered Bernette's entry into 'our jewelled village'. She introduced her as 'sans man' at the W.I., 'partnerless' at University of the Third Age gatherings, and 'a singleton' at the Bridge Club. At each venue, budgerigar-Bernette admitted never marrying any of the eligible men who pursued her, and outliving them all.

'I related, but never relented,' she said mysteriously.

Miriam assumed she'd pecked them all to death.

'I've had my adventures' was all Bernette would say. 'I've been *enriched*. Tuhuhuh!'

Lucky old budgie, thought Miriam, surprised that anyone with mystique, anyone *enriched*, should want to drink tea in a shabby little house like hers.

A bone-dry laugh - Elspeth - pierced the kitchen door. Elspeth had no mystique at all. To Miriam, she was a mean widow on a generous pension, abhorring change yet following it slavishly. When Miriam strayed into 'lounge' and 'serviette', Elspeth was in clover. She could bemoan the decline of the English language while providing the necessary corrections ['sitting rum and nepkin these days, deahr'], and quietly look down her long nose at Miriam and the ignoramuses she represented.

'I sharpen her teeth', thought Miriam.

Yank, went the invisible string, and Miriam's eyes jerked towards that damn spot of grease on the microwave. Not a random smear, but a clear silhouette of a human face, in profile, as if someone had painted it there, or carved it like a cameo in the congealed grease. The perky nose, full lower lip, high forehead - and that distinctive round shape of the skull.

Oh yes, it's your face, Miriam.

That's what you're seeing.

It's you.

Miriam Marble-Head, they called her at school. So long ago, but remembered still, those sniggers whenever the geometry teacher said 'circumference'. Miriam Marble-Head, Q.E.D.

Marble-shaped her head remained, and marble-shaped, perk-nosed and full-lipped was the greasy silhouette she stared at on the microwave's shiny-white metal door.

‘Require any help, Miriam, tuhuh?’ twittered Bernette.

‘Not inextricably jemmed in, are you, deahr?’ added Elspeth. ‘Huck!’

‘Nearly there’, Miriam sang back, peering at her silhouette while shovelling cut-price shortbread into the biscuit barrel, and opening the microwave door.

*

In the rota’s infancy, Miriam began on that very first Tuesday with leaf tea and wholemeal biscuits from the farmers’ market. Two days later, behind her thick spectacles, fury blazed.

On Wednesday, at Bernette’s house, Miriam’s biscuits were finessed by a giant hill of scones with full-fruit jam, and a patronisingly large pot of clotted cream.

By four-o-clock on Thursday, Elspeth had trumped them both, her mahogany table creaking beneath the weight of petit-fours, crust-free sandwiches, and those expensive mini-patisseries from that posh Italian place on the High Street. Petrocammelli’s, was it? No, Miriam was thinking of petro-chemicals. Elspeth’s husband had been in petro-chemicals. Sold them? Bought them? *Drank* them for all she cared.

To save the world from starvation, Bernette had resorted to flattery.

‘Oh Elspeth, this is so *you*, but the expense, it’s too-too unfair a burden my dear. *Tuhuhuh!*’

Elspeth consented, regally, and they settled for tea and

biscuits and a warm scone, three times a week. Miriam's dislike of scones swelled over the months into a deep, burning hatred.

And now here she was, warming them.

In the microwave.

She dragged her gaze away from the silhouette.

'Miriam-marble-head, you're losing your marbles', she said. 'Fancy thinking a smear of fat could be a picture of *you*!'

But didn't someone crack open a walnut and find the face of Christ? Or was it Gandhi? Or Frank Sinatra? –

'Having trouble with the milk, Miriam? Udder problems? A reluctant cow, concealed in the utility room? Tuhuh!'

'Huckhuck! Huck!'

I'd like to hucking-well conceal them in the utility room, mused Miriam. *In the chest freezer. Butchered and boned and labelled 'mutton'!*

'Stop! Stop!' hissed a voice in her head. 'Such wicked thoughts! Those large-print books from the mobile library, they're altogether too *modern* for you!'

Except the voice wasn't hers.

She closed her eyes and saw a huge slab of Bernette-scone, smothered in Elspeth-butter, and she hated it.

*

Nibbling at her unloved, dry scone, she listened to Elspeth's account of the balanced flue being fitted to her brand new, high efficiency gas boiler.

'*Such* incompetents, my plumbers! Tweedledum and Tweedledee, the smelly-overall-men from hell! Huck-huck! *And* they *smoke*! Is it *allowed*? Even the reprobates who mended the *chemney* didn't smoke! Huck!'

Bernette countered with a paean to all-electric.

'It's so clean, and barely a moving part. I can't recommend it enough. Switch on, switch off. Click, and click again!'

Miriam, whose ancient, rusty boiler was oil-fired, heard only 'enough'. She drifted into a scone-less, leaf-tea-fuelled daydream...

Gas.
Electricity.
Oil.

Did that sum up the three of them?

Miriam dreaded the gassy spasms hissing from Elspeth's horse-lips. Yet, by seizing the chance to organise the presence of others, Elspeth was rarely alone. She always had people to poison.

Budgerigar-Bernette brought an electric spark to village life, and was equally popular with males and females of a certain age. Widowers were drawn to her side at every barn-dance and bring and buy sale, as if she had an electro-magnetic field hidden in her handbag. Female singletons hovered at its edge, waiting to pounce on stray males, whether rejected, resting, or electrically recharged. At village gatherings, high-voltage Bernette topped the invitation list.

Not so Miriam.

She was an afterthought. She had energy, once, but it drifted away. Why, where, she knew not. Miriam was 'pleasant'. Diplomatic. 'Oil on troubled waters'. Oil. A pleasant little splash of diplomatic bloody oil!

She glanced at the syncopated lips of Elspeth and Bernette. *Why in heavens name do they want me here?*

Briefly, she envied them.

Elspeth and Bernette's singleton-status was at least past tense. They hadn't always been man-less, like Miriam. Bernette and Elspeth seemed…richer. Not financially. Money was just *there*. Or, in Miriam's case, not.

'Richer'? Or…what was Bernette's word? *Enriched*? Miriam would never be described as enriched.

She's not a great talker, the village would say, but she's nice.

She can't organise, but she's nice.

She's not electric, but she's nice.

Not *enriched*, no, but nice.

Nice.

Fury swelled behind Miriam's spectacles. If she had an old scone for every bloody '*nice*' she'd overheard, the hardened pile of projectiles would ensure a painful death *by stoning* of this twittering, hucking and judging old pair, pecking and prancing in her down-at-heel lounge, preening and grazing amidst the threadbare furnishings, disapproving of the teacups and the teapot and the teaspoons and the tea!

Miriam blinked, to control her fury.

No. It's envy, she reminded herself.

Envy.

And Bitterness.

And now Bitchiness too.

Miriam, is this what Tuesdays have become?

*

For the second time, a screech from Bernette electrocuted Miriam's daydream. Each twist of Elspeth's plumber's wrench seemed to tighten Bernette's vocal chords. Did Miriam have over-sensitive hearing?

She didn't think so.

She almost mentioned the spot of grease when it was her turn to talk. She got a turn, on Tuesdays, because it was her house. Miriam opted for safer ground.

'I've just realised we're all on different fuels, yes? You're Gas. You're Electricity. I'm Oil. Strange, isn't it?'

Her tea-companions gave her a puzzled look.

'Oh yes, deahr,' agreed Elspeth, concisely.

'And difference needs to be allowed for, Miriam, surely?'

A bare pause signalled the end of her turn, and the screeching and braying resumed with more tales of what-plumbers-keep-in-their-overalls. At least she'd been given a turn. On Wednesdays and Thursdays Miriam was Any Other Business, saying so little she wondered why she was there at all.

As an audience perhaps? A witness, somehow validating the hollow chatter of Elspeth and Bernette? And to make the meetings quorate. Three's company, but two gives rise to gossip.

And *one*?

Miriam had always been a 'one'.

'One is one and all alone and ever more shall be so', she hummed to herself.

Did being alone make you see your own likeness in a smear of grease? She almost asked them, but could guess the response. Elspeth would be poisonously glad that house-room was being given to grease.

'What next, Miriam? Mice? *Rets*?'

And Bernette would screech: 'Dear me, Miriam, you're in dreamland! Grease one minute, a Rembrandt the next! You imagined it, dear. Just imagined it. Tuhuhuh! It's not really there. It's merely grrrrrease.'

When they left, Miriam bolted the door.

'I'm *enriching* my safety!' she snapped.

Piling dishes into the sink, she turned on the tap so hard it spat. Her scarcely-nibbled scone rocketed across the kitchen into the bin. Guilt for the world's starving masses was squashed by a Tuesday fury.

In a string-snapping moment she thrust a cloth into the suds and moved to wipe the grease from the microwave's harsh metal side. It *was* just grease, not a painted silhouette of her ridiculous, marble-round head.

Bernette would have been right. She imagined it.

*

'I doubt we can achieve much more, Bernette. Don't you agree?' asked Elspeth, as they strolled away from Miriam's tiny cottage towards two grander versions.

'I do, Elspeth. But 'achieve' is correct. The house is clean again. Miriam seems to have rediscovered her routines. She's *drifting* far less.'

Elspeth nodded, counting further improvements onto four bony fingers.

'She's tidied the garden. I peeped at the utility room and it's no longer in chaos. She's replaced that dangerous microwave - the one with the lethal wiring. *And* she's beginning to converse.'

Bernette pulled a face. 'She's *talking*, Elspeth. Let's not call it conversation yet.'

'No, no, of course. But she *is* following the thread. Goodness me, the things I've uttered, just to trigger *some* sort of reaction.'

'Both of us, Elspeth. Mea culpa too.'

'At least she's seeing patterns now. 'Gas, Electricity, Oil'. Remember? She's alert again. She's observing.'

'Elspeth, my dear, I'm relieved,' said Bernette as they went their separate ways. 'I've so lost my love of scones.'

*

Lifting the soapy cloth, Miriam realised she'd squeezed it bone-dry in her furious fist. She flung it again at the suds.

And squeezed it dry again.

Yes, she *did* imagine it...

'Miriam', she said, 'you *imagined* it!'

And she dropped the dishcloth on the floor, wiped her hands on the tail of her Tuesday cardigan, and headed for the newly-tidied utility room.

Miriam quickly found it - shoved away in an old wooden box since the day she'd stopped...imagining. She lifted the lid, and shook hands with a long-lost friend.

Not bothering to protect the kitchen table, she began.

How long it took she didn't know. What did time matter? Nobody would call, and the dishes could soak themselves clean. She stood up to survey the outcome, as she had done so many times in a past almost forgotten.

The oil paints seemed unaffected by age, the brushes supple, and the canvas, a harsh white screen when she'd begun, displayed something close to the image she'd suddenly, viscerally needed to create.

As a portrait, it was...workmanlike.

'*Yes, Elspeth, naïve*', she said, to no-one.

'But it's *me*.'

Miriam had painted her own round face - bumps, blemishes, spectacles, truth and all - as a reflection in the shiny glass door of the microwave. In the background, over her shoulder, the wall-clock in the mirror-image showed time moving in reverse.

The vanishing point was the late afternoon horizon, framed by the kitchen window and glimpsed through tangles of apple-green leaves and the scarlet buds of a rambling rose.

As an afterthought, Miriam brushed a marble-shaped

smear of paint onto the bright white image of the microwave door.

In her second realisation of the day, she knew she must act, before the opportunity drifted away, as so many had before. She phoned the helpdesk of the local Learning Centre. Though just about to leave, the lady was helpfulness itself. And what a pleasant voice, Miriam thought, as they discussed options and levels.

'Oil Painting classes, please', she said with enthusiasm.

They were on Tuesday afternoons, and the dying fall of an old loyalty silenced her.

Dare she disturb an arrangement so militarily planned by Elspeth? Dare she close the cage on Bernette? If she upset them would they snigger behind her back at the farmer's market in the High Street? What if she bumped into them in the tight confines of the mobile library?

Or if they simply ignored her?

She stared at the truth of her self-portrait, at its ageing face against the fading horizon. Truth returned her stare. Do realisations come in threes? she asked herself, as the faces of her tea-companions floated into her head - and floated away again.

'They don't belong here, Miriam', she said. "They're gas, electricity. And you are oil - *nice* oil. A pleasant splash of nice, diplomatic oil.'

She would try to find her voice, and talk with Elspeth and Bernette as adults. She would explain.

She would thank them.

Yes, she was oil.

'Tuesdays? Oh dear.'

'*Press on, Miriam, press on*', said a new voice. '*There will be tea and biscuits - but no scones - at the Learning Centre. And there will be other people.*'

'No...No, Tuesdays are *fine*', she said.

Lapsang Souchong

Roses are deceitful.

Prune them, hard, said page 23 of his know-it-all gardening book. Page 24 advised sharp secateurs, stout gloves, long sleeves. True to form, he didn't read page 24. The roses mugged him, forearms a trackway of blood.

He counted his wounds in the abrasive garden, an upturned bucket for a seat and a monstrous yew hedge shielding the barely-trodden lane beyond. One of his few unscratched body parts, his ear, detected the hubbub of new neighbours tramping past. Well, *he* was new so they were new to him.

I should introduce myself, but with a tower of boxes to unpack, and a 'garden' to tame…

'Shitty little cur! Homunculus! Nasty, brutish - and *ridiculously* short!'

An angry voice, the wife presumably. *Were* they married? They *sounded* married. Then a different sound. A cry. A man. And the stomach-turning noise of a stick hitting bone. Should I be spying on hot-blooded neighbours I've never met? He peered through an evergreen gash, instantly ducking as a walking stick whooshed at the sky and swung shockingly down.

But not, after all, at him. A male hand - the husband's he assumed - slapped it away from his white-haired skull. The woman looked stronger than the man. No, won't introduce myself, just yet.

He crept back to his roses, the clamour waning as his neighbours jousted along a weed-heavy path and into their castle. No portcullis rattled down, the slam of a heavy door being drawbridge enough.

He envied those who could afford detached.

Or afford a gardener. A deceitful rose-thorn, drill-bit sharp, daggered into his thumb, to the bone. Pain, blood. And how much blood does a bloody thumb hold? Or not hold, because blood was surging out, unstoppably. He peeled off his already-reddened glove and the blood flowed faster still, as if drawn to daylight. His handkerchief proved useless, white turning rapidly red, a hot fainting red. He stumbled indoors, ran the tap. The white porcelain blushed scarlet. First-aid kit? Yes, in the unpacked tower of boxes, take your pick.

The fall-back, a pasty-green teacloth, matched his pallor till it too turned scarlet and he stumbled half-thinking down one garden path and up the next, red-green teacloth fumbling at the maybe-not-neighbourly doorbell. It rang, as darker thumb-blood pumped down his palm and wrist.

'*BLOOD*! All over my door!' Her first words. 'How did you manage *that*?' She pointed a finger at his pulsing thumb.

'Roses...Rose-thorn.' Mumbling, faint. 'Taming the garden. Failing.' She looked squarely at him, over sharp spectacles.

'*Failing*? But screw your courage to the sticking-place and we'll not fail!'

He recognised the reference, from Shakespeare at school. Good morning, Lady Macbeth. Did Mr Macbeth survive the swish of your stick? Wobbling now.

'Should've called round, introduce myself. Heard you...go past...' Woozy. Voice a blur. 'Can't stop the bleeding...'

In the iron curtain pause, he understood what a rarely-crossed threshold this was. To contradict, she flung open the door and dragged him in.

'Gerald! *Gerald!* Neighbour! Self-inflicted wound!'

No sign of Gerald, Gerald Macbeth, only a loud clacking from the dark-red hallway - a sound he hadn't heard in years, the beats and clicks of an old typewriter. She followed his eyes.

'Writing', she said. 'Well, *typing*. It's a Remington. Clickety-clack. As antique as the rest of us. *Gerald! Now!*'

Oof, strong lungs - and disdain. Without preamble, she raised his ridiculous, tea-towelled thumb high in the air and disappeared to the kitchen, leaving him in the dark-red hallway, a bloodied schoolboy seeking Miss Macbeth's permission to go to the lav. But, yes, the thumb bled more slowly. He heard the scrape of a kettle amid the unrelenting tack-tack-tack of invisible fingers jabbing at a keyboard.

Woozy still, he collided with an old umbrella-stand, a porcupine of sharp canes and brollies. Was one of these jutting spines the stick that Lady Mac whacked her husband with? Aloft, his thumb pulsed like a warning beacon.

Scanning the dark hall, he found himself staring at the short leather frame of, he presumed, Gerald Macbeth of the Remington.

'You'll be The Neighbour. Mm? Self-inflicted wound?'

'Er...'

'Good name, that, 'The Neighbour'. Collectable. Don't be put out if I call you The Neighbour.'

'My name's -'

'No. Don't tell. I like The Neighbour. As a name. In my head.' He twirled his index finger against his skull. 'Rosamunde mention the writing?'

'Um, I think she called it *typing*? The Rem - '

The hallway darkened in the gaffe-silence, but blood flowed from thumb to cheeks, and the throbbing decreased. Gerald's leather face became a one-eyed glare. He flicked a peremptory hand at the sitting room door and strode through. If he noticed the ridiculous tea-towelled thumb saluting the ceiling, he gave no sign. The Neighbour tottered after him, ducking his arm gingerly beneath the architrave.

'You might have invited our neighbour to sit *down*', she said, entering, tea-tray in hand.

'By the way, my name's -'

'Sit, sit, there,' she said, nodding at a battered Queen Anne chair. 'Gerald. Exert yourself by pouring tea. Too much to ask?'

How old was she? Quick, smooth. Age-spotted hands juggled clean bandages, a bottle of something pungent, wads of cotton wool. Lady Florence Macbeth Nightingale now, pulling his absurd raised arm down towards her like the handle on a slot-machine.

'You're a lucky man', sneered Gerald. She's good with *blood*. Ex-Nurse. Armed Forces. Seen it all, eh, Rosamunde?'

'And saw it again, in the Falklands. Blood a-plenty - but not from rose-thorns. Yours, though, was a bayonet.' She swabbed and wrapped, dropping wet red discards into a plastic bag. Gerald's sneer became a question.

'Don't suppose he'll ever see a *bullet* wound, eh?'

'Oh dear,' she said, dismissing the question with a scissor snip. 'You've upset poor Gerald. Calls people 'he' when they upset him. Or *she*. If they're still in the room, of course. Which we are.'

Gerald spoon-tapped his teacup. Lady Mac's spectacles threw a vat-of-acid glance, etching the tappety Macbeth into silence. Red-white swabs swam inside the plastic bag like intestines.

'He' wondered why his strange hosts chose to live together in a loathing so palpable you could prune it with a pair of secateurs.

Oh, for a detached house, moated, rose-free.

Despite himself, he rang the doorbell again, bloodlessly this time. Lady Macbeth, doubling as the Porter, swung back the hinges.

'Er, I never said thank you yesterday, for...' He semaphored with his thumb. 'Brought you a little token, nothing really.'

She peered at the caddy of lapsang souchong tea, nodded, drew him into the dark-red hallway.

'Timely,' she said. 'The kettle's on. *Gerald*! *He*'s here again!'

No Gerald, just clack-tack-clack from the Remington. She pointed to the Queen Anne chair, and The Neighbour obediently sat as the kettle screeched. Hunting scenes dangled from the anaglypta, askew. He turned to examine the window-sill scattered with dead spiders, and instead examined the leather face of Gerald, catapulted upwards from his lair beneath the sofa-springs.

'Been fiddling with an idea, ever since…' He wobbled his finger at the bandaged thumb. 'Tell me: get a *tetanus* jab, did you?'

'Er…?'

'Ahah, you didn't! It's a killer, you know, tetanus.'

'Er, is it?'

'Can be *fatal*. That's the idea I'm fiddling with.'

Gerald stared hard at The Neighbour now.

'Show you something', Gerald said, leaping up in his unexpectedly sudden way. Drawing The Neighbour down the dark hallway into a box-room, he jabbed a finger at a gunmetal filing cabinet. With a flick, he was riffling through the top drawer, extracting one grey manuscript after another and as quickly flipping them back.

'Scenarios. Treatments. For TV. Or for 'the movies', as they insist on calling *film* these days. Lost count of how many. 'Inventing events', I call it. Plausible events - in *my* view. Your tetanus plot's in here, for now.'

He rammed the 'Pending' drawer closed. The drawer below said 'Maybes'. 'Rejections' sat hopelessly beneath.

The Neighbour wondered where the ideas began, since Gerald looked like he'd struggle to invent yesterday's date. A kettle hissed in the kitchen.

'*Daydreams*, according to *her*', said Gerald, pointing. The filing cabinet rang metallically in response to his kick.

'Where are *my* dreams?' she asks, cracked bloody record. 'Where's *my* mystery, Gerald? Where's *my* buzz?' *Buzz?* What kind of word is 'buzz'? Gets it from her bonkers Army cronies, fidget-fidget, waiting for a war. *Buzz!* What am I, a bloody bumble-bee? *We*'ll show *her*. The witch.'

'*We*?' The Neighbour thought. Leave me out of it.

Tea, in a faded china cup, was...

'Civilised, Gerald. See? And *very* fine lapsang.' She raised her cup, dipping her head in thanks. '*And* it's the only tea Gerald won't adulterate with whisky. Doubly welcome.'

Silence groaned loudly.

'Shown you the bulging filing cabinet, has he?'

The Neighbour's eyebrows gave the game away.

'Thought as much. Bulging because nobody *buys*. Were you *ever* a breadwinner, Gerald, remind me? Bread*loser*, more like.'

Gerald humphed. The Neighbour burrowed into the springs of the Queen Anne chair.

'And *surely* he mentioned 'invented events'? He says it in his *sleep*. Alas, no invented *man* who pays invented cash for daydreams - cash to spend on fine lapsang, every day, not once a millennium when a wayward rose-thorn lacerates a thumb.'

She raised her lapsang to her lips, and Gerald ducked in with a pennyworth of his own.

'Loose tea, was it? Or tea-bags?'

She glared. 'You insult our visitor, Gerald. Tea bags indeed!'

'Damn!' said Gerald. 'That might put the kybosh on it.'

'Um, on what exactly?' There, thought the Neighbour, I got a word in.

'On the idea.' Gerald twirled a finger against his skull. 'The scenario. For 'the movies.''

Rosamunde sighed. Gerald's unlikely bucket sank deeper into the well.

'Try this,' he said. 'Opening scene, English pastoral music. Camera pans: thorny red rosebush, pair of delicate hands - the victim's - shiny secateurs. Hands begin to prune, snip-snip, then - 'Ouch! Damn!' Strident music now - pricked his thumb, but innocent, yes?'

'Er...'

'*Ah*, but Mr Villain is watching - gap in the hedge. Fast forward for you here: murder mystery, touch of gothic. Popular genre, agreed?'

'Er...?'

'Next: Villain distils *tetanus*. Don't ask me how, haven't doodled the detail. Taste concealed with lapsang souchong. Smoky enough I imagine, if tetanus *has* any taste? Buggered if I know. Good cinematics, regardless.'

At the mention of tea, Rosamunde loudly drained her lapsang.

'Where was I? Yes. Villain's fingers inject tetanus into tea-bags, and into a caddy they go. Close-up on same fingers forming a fist. Cross-fade to fist on neighbour's door - rap-tap-tap - like your knuckles on ours, yes?'

The Neighbour wanted to say, 'no, *I* rang the bell, bloodied it', but Gerald was off again.

'Door opens, victim surprised. 'Neighbourly gift for you, old chap. A token, nothing really. Best quality lapsang." You follow?'

Gerald ignored The Neighbour's struggle to sift fiction from fact.

'Cut to *victim*'s kitchen, extreme close-up on *his* hands - one bandaged, hint of blood. T'other dropping deadly tea-bags into warmed pot. Workable, yes?'

Rosamunde's eyeballs gutted the ceiling. Gerald motored on.

'Mortuary slab: close up on victim's hand; rose-thorn puncture deeper than a mineshaft. Ahah, tetanus poisoning! Used to call it lock-jaw.'

'The ignorant still do', spat Rosamunde. Gerald shrugged her off.

'Flashback then: victim flexes jaw. Never had an anti-tet injection in his life - tut-tut. Medical records prove it. Flash forward: camera on Coroner's face. '*Accidental death*', say his lips. More English Pastoral. Roll credits.'

Gerald raised his lapsang. 'Perfect murder,' he said, between slurps. 'Who needs bullets when a rose can kill?'

Rosamunde groaned. 'And just *how* does one distil tetanus? Mm? Isn't it a bacterium? *Daydreams*!'

'There's life, Rosamunde - and there's art. Not always the twain etcetera.'

'*Art*?'

She makes it sound like a gob of phlegm, the Neighbour thought.

'There's neither art nor *life* in this! Your 'Mr Villain' - *ridiculous* - he pops on latex gloves, I suppose? Locates his tetanus tweezers? Snaps up tiny tiddles of bacteria that happen to be lolling about?'

'It's *workable*, dammit! And it needn't be a '*He*.''

'*It*, then.'

'Or *She*!' spat Gerald.

'*It* pops them into a test-tube? Squirts multi-purpose liquid from a pipette? *Clichés*!'

Seconds out! thought The Neighbour, as Gerald returned the punch.

'Ye-es, pipette, test-tube, face-mask! Visual, mysterious. *It* gives the blood-red liquid a swirl, to eerie laboratory music -'

'Preposterou -'

'- *And* if *It* is a *She,* she could be a *witch!* A tea-drinking witch with a warty nose and an incantation!'

The bell - spoon on teacup - had no effect. Rosamunde boxed on.

'Oh, definitely an incantation, Gerald. *Death to Men*! That should do!'

'Death to Men, Ro? We've been dead for years. *Women* killed us!'

What's worse, the Neighbour thought, the sarcasm or the scenario? Rosamunde knew. Her pert lips stretched into a sneer. Had she been a dragon - and perhaps in some invented event she was - ropes of fire would explode from her wrath-filled nostrils. The Neighbour imagined Gerald's body melting on the charred sofa, teaspoon gripped in what remained of his blackened tappety hand.

'Mind you, if the perpetrator *is* a She,' said Gerald, 'then '*Death to Men*' is workable, I'll give you that.'

Lady Mac turned her spectacles on The Neighbour. 'How blessed you are,' she said. 'The first Man in thirty years to witness Gerald giving me *anything*. You must call again.'

In fact, they called on him.

Unannounced.

He was up a stepladder, painting hair and ceiling with his non-bandaged hand. He cursed through boxes towards the doorbell, thumb stained with emulsion in lieu of blood. Did they say, 'we'll come back when it's more convenient'? No. They stood there, till he let them in. At least they've jogged my memory, he thought, adding an anti-tetanus jab to the long to-do list. He shifted pots of filler from the coffee-table, dragged dustsheets from the few chairs he owned.

My only visitors. Get a life.

While the kettle hummed, he learned of his predecessor.

'*Disappeared*? Er, how? Why?'

'In arrears. With the rent,' Gerald explained. 'Some sort of writer. Murder, horror, suchlike. Swopped a few ideas, he and I... No, no, barely saw him, eh, Ro?'

'*You* showed him your filing cabinet, as I recall.' Ignoring Gerald's 'humph!' she stared through the window, at the impenetrable hedge. 'An occasional glimpse. Little is seen, here...'

'Landlord saw neither him *nor* the rent', quipped Gerald. Dropping his voice to a whisper, he added, 'And not the first tenant to disappear from…' He twirled a mysterious finger at The Neighbour's house.

'Moonlight flits,' explained Rosamunde, fluttering a bony hand as if to launch a broomstick.

'Bailiffs had the nerve to knock on *our* door' said Gerald. 'Enormous chaps. Asked if *we*'d got the last one! Never knew his *name*! Always called him The Neighb-'

'Sad,' snapped Rosamunde, without looking it.

'Never had *tea* with the fellow,' chirped Gerald, reminding his host the kettle had boiled.

The Neighbour had gifted his only tea. The cupboard held a few dregs of decaff. I wish the bottle of whisky was in the bloody cupboard too, he thought. Gerald's radar was pinging it, ten fingers tapping his chair in hope of golden glassfuls.

'You *do* intend to stay longer than your predecessor?' asked Rosamunde. 'No moonlight flit, I hope?'

Her question warmed him. Hope was rarely thrown his way. The run-down house, bought at auction with suspicious ease, was everything he had. Yes, staying.

'I only have coffee,' he said. Gerald's fingers screeched to a halt. 'Um...or there's whisky? If you'd prefer?'

He was relieved when they left, not because the bottle was empty but because he was. They'd gutted him for his meagre life-story. He learned nothing of theirs. We *insist* you knock on our door tomorrow, have tea with us, they said.

Out of loneliness, he did, forgetfully thumbing the bell with a strangely painful hand, arm, shoulder too.

Rosamunde snapped open the door, ushering him in, silently clicking the latch behind them. The Queen Anne chair awaited, tea things lurking on the scratched side-board.

'The lapsang's just for you,' she said. 'Returning your kindness.'

The Neighbour's smoky tea tasted stronger than before. Rosamunde stirred her lemon tisane. Golden whisky swirled in Gerald's chipped crystal glass.

With his good hand, the Neighbour raised a china cup. All three sipped, as the room eased to stillness - so still he heard the faint jib-pause-jab of the wall-clock dangling from the anaglypta. Its faint pulse stroked his memory back to his first visit: sweat on his skin; his own pulse faint; thorn-pierced thumb staining an improvised bandage with rose-red blood that almost turned to black.

Strange, mused the Neighbour, how a cold memory of sweat can feel so real. He swallowed more tea, feeling its welcome warmth against the cold tightness of his jaw. Gerald's whisky winked questions at the ceiling. Rosamunde's fingers squeezed the throat of her hot tisane.

Jib. Jab. Jib. Jab.

The Neighbour's penny dropped. My hosts, they *detest* lapsang souchong! Drank it to be polite. Well, more for me.

Jib. Jab. Jib. Jab.

The tea's steamy smoke became a fog. On the dust-covered sill, dead spiders morphed into lobsters longer than arms. Daubed hunting scenes severed their rusty wires and orbited the room, as a sludge of Pendings, Rejections, Maybes seeped from three hard metal drawers, bleeding into the sump of a single invented event.

Such puncturing smiles, my hosts, thought The Neighbour, as the tick of time took its leave, sucking the clock from the sitting-room wall, its faint jib-jab swamped by a hard tock-tack as the unmistakeable Remington started up behind a distant door, unknown fingers rapping at the brute keys, drilling black ink into paper whiter than ice.

Body rigid in the Queen Anne chair, the Neighbour's locked neck could not turn beyond the sharp smiles of Gerald and Ro, could not turn towards the sound - tack-*tack*, tack-*tack* - the unseen mad machine laugh-*clacking,* laugh-*clacking, clack-tack-clack,* from behind the still-closed door at the end of the dark-red hallway, so dark now it was turning entirely to black.

Old Man, Young Pub

Frank detested his name.

He wasn't especially frank, but he *was* Frank Smith - printed in black and white on his birth certificate. Not that he could find it. Not that he had much call for it anymore.

'What sort of name did you *expect*?' Lucy used to ask him. '*Dirk Stallion*? *You*?'

Dream on, Frank Smith. World record boring name. He sipped his pint.

How long had he been drinking in *The Blue Anchor*? Forty years? Mm, and the rest. And why call a pub *The Blue Anchor* when the nearest sea is...?

Must be closer than you think, Frank, because your beer tastes of salt tonight.

He'd managed to nab his own barstool for once. But how can you get comfy with that bloody juke-box chucking out clattery songs?

Songs?

Squawk, more like. Saucepan lids rattling on pots of jabber.

And *young* jabber, tonight. This lot, can they be old enough to drink? Must be thirty of them, jeans and beards and T-shirts mucking up the carpet. Screechy young women too, jabbering 'Sooo kind', when a scruffy student buys them a glass of plonk.

Jabbering, Frank. But none of them jabbering to you.

Two barstools along, *used* to be Pete Booth, from the Market. Prostate cancer. Adjacent stool was dear old Barry Brunt.

Electrician, just as you were, Frank.

You used to compare notes, swop kit, double up on big re-wiring jobs. Double up on pints too. And you doubled up on Barry's sister, eh, because you married her - Lucy. Lucy Brunt, as was. After courting, it was Frank and Lucy…Smith.

He hoped she'd take to pubs, hoped she'd like *The Blue Anchor,* but she never did. Not like Barry.

'To be fair, Frank, they talked straight, at the hospital. My meter's run out,' Barry said, lifting the last defiant pint he'd ever savour. 'Any day now, my switch clicks from on to off.'

Poor Lucy though. Her switch took twice as long as Barry's. Nor, god help us, was it quiet. Frank Smith still heard the pain, in their silent empty house. They'd never got on. Fifty years married, and never got on. Different wishes and wants. Now, in their empty bed, if he managed to sleep at all, he prayed not to dream.

These noisy pubs, Frank, that Lucy never liked, they take the edge off.

Two younger bottoms squatted on the bar-stools now. Students, a beard each, supping lager. He'd stopped listening in, each word longer than the one before. *In-com-prehen-sible.* Sixteen letters, in yesterday's crossword that he couldn't do.

Another blast of noise as the pub door flung in more grubby T-shirts, the men in trousers made of stuff that didn't even look like cloth. The women? Wearing close to bugger all. Jabber and cackle, louder now. There must be a bloke outside gets commission for pushing folk in off the street - if they've got loud beards and they're wearing black like at a…

A new arrival jostled Frank's elbow as he raised his glass, splashing beer down his tie. Waste of bloody beer. Waste of a tie too, he thought, with this lot.

'Sorry, mate. Didn't see you.'

No. Nobody sees Frank Smith. Invisible Man with the boring name. Used-to-be-electrician-widower. His beer tastes of salt, and it's staining his nice clean tie.

Frank eased old legs to the floor, plonking his undone crossword on the stool as a marker. He shuffled through the prattling crowd, in Charlie Chaplin turns, past arms and elbows to the haven of the loo. To wash off spilt beer.

Because, Frank, salt can stain.

*

The return trip was a breeze. Elbows and beards were gone, the jabber stilled to silence. An old couple sipped quiet halves at a window table.

That might have been me and Luce, if she'd taken to pubs. It was mostly only me.

At the almost-empty bar, the sad bod who worked in the petrol station stared at his phone, one slow finger rolling the screen up, down, up, down. All Frank could hear was the clock tick.

The Blue Anchor? Huh, no need of an anchor in here! It's a bloody stagnant pond!

Stale.

Flat.

Silent.

Like at home.

He sipped beer that didn't even taste of salt.

New, the barman. Well, Frank *thought* it was a man. Long hair in a pony-tail; bones like a mannequin; a set of porcelain cheeks.

'Where's everybody gone?'

The barman didn't look up from his paper. A finger jerked from his mannequin-frame, twirled twice in the air and jabbed at a poster near the door. Bloody mime artist, thought Frank. The poster was too small. He struggled back to his feet, and shuffled closer.

What A Performance!
Plays for Pubs!
Tonight: Krapp's Last Tape!

Bring your drink, it said. Frank had never heard of *Krapp's Last Tape*. He peered at the small print, harder to read these days.

'A one-act play by Samuel...Buckett.'

Never heard of him. He shuffled back to the bar, waggling his empty glass.

'Pint 'o bitter?'

Frank nodded. *Why not change your name to Pint of Bitter, Frank?*

'This play thing,' he said, flicking a finger at the poster. 'Where is it? Says it's at *The Blue Anchor.* But that's *here.*'

The barman placed a full pint on the bar, jerking a thumb to the left.

'Next door,' he said.

'Next door? That's the skittle-alley, next door.'

'Used to be', said the barman. 'No-one wants to play, these days.'

Humph. I would. If I could bend down that far.

'Make more cash renting it out,' said the barman. 'Bands, craft-fairs. Plays. This theatre lot, they've booked it every week, for the foreseeable.' He looked at his watch. 'Starts in five', he said, and loped off to serve the sad bod from the petrol station, whose free hand waved an empty glass in lieu of a white flag.

Frank wobbled back to the poster. *Krapp's Last Tape*?

'Huh, can't even spell 'crap'', he mumbled, to no-one. 'And this Krapp, has he a first name? Maybe it's *Frank,* Frank? *Frank Krapp.* Almost as bad as *Frank Smith.*'

He wobbled back to the bar, but didn't sit. Pete and Bernie's stools were empty, the old couple gone, and petrol station man was marooned inside his phone. Frank's beer tasted of silence now.

'How much is it?' he called to the barman. A pony-tailed face stared at the sports page while heading an imaginary football at the poster. Once more, Frank shuffled to the small print.

Pay only what you think we're worth!

'Pay nowt, then', said Frank, and with paper and pint in hand, he shuffled next door to a long thin theatre, once the skittle-alley of *The Blue Anchor*.

A young woman, dressed all in black, whispered a welcome. He nearly didn't see her, nearly walked through her, it was so dark - like The Odeon, at Saturday matinees when he was a kid. Memory flashed him an image: the sudden change from empty sunshine to a darkness full of heroes. The young woman fussed him to the edge of the back-row, in a new silence.

When his eyes grew accustomed to the space, he saw he'd got the last seat. Fifty of us, he guessed, scanning the rows in front of him. No wonder the pub emptied. In the darkness, he heard slurps a-plenty as glasses met lips. The lights came up on a little stage made of rough wooden blocks painted black, where a rough wooden ball used to knock down nine-pins.

Even when lit, the stage was dark. He counted the plugs and wires dangling from the lanterns and, an electrician's habit, traced them back from the lighting bar to a crude junction box fitted to the wall. An inch this side of legal, he thought.

Might get out alive.

He waited for more actors to enter, but there was only one, an old clown of a man, called Krapp. He had an old-fashioned tape-recorder, reel-to-reel, and a box of old tapes, which he played while eating a banana and banging on about something and nothing. It's like Desert Island Discs, Frank thought. But there's no music, just a voice, and the memories on the tapes are...*crap*.

Pay only what you think we're worth? He'd definitely pay nowt for *this*!

I come in here to get away from an old man - me! - in an empty pub full of memories, and I end up watching an old man's memories on an empty stage in the pub's old skittle-alley. And there's all this silence, all these pauses. I thought he'd forgotten his lines at first.

Pause. Silence. Frank took a silent sip of beer. Barman, pint of Lonely Bitter, please.

Krapp, the old man, was going on about women, women from the past - or the younger Krapp's voice was, on the tape.

Well, Frank, at our age, me and Krapp, the past is what there is.

At least he had an unobstructed view, even from the back row. The young woman who'd ushered him in was standing against the side wall, a few feet away. He realised, with a tingle of guilt, she must've given him the seat reserved for her.

Krapp wandered off. Backstage, a cork popped from a bottle, a soda siphon squirted, then Krapp returned, tipsy. Everyone laughed.

Everyone except Frank.

One old man recognised another.

When Krapp mumbled something about being a stupid bastard thirty years ago, Frank wanted to scream at the young audience, wanted to yell at them through the silence, *'we were all stupid bastards thirty years ago.'*

The old reel-to-reel kept playing bits of the same tape, stopping and fast-forwarding. Some babble about Krapp and a woman in a punt on a stream, and the water moving beneath the boat, moving it side to side, forward and back, forward and back, like the tape.

And forward and back, forward and back went Frank, re-winding, remembering - him and Lucy, just turned twenty-one, rowing on the lake in the public park, in their courting days. Barry Brunt's sister, pretty Lucy Brunt. And mooring up, invisible beneath the willow trees, in the deep shade. And proposing. And Lucy Brunt accepting, and oh, my goodness, what followed that day, that night, what followed.

But knowing, here, now, in the long thin silent dark, that so much more could have come of it.

Then Frank was fumbling in his pocket for a hankie. Ridiculous, in the old skittle-alley of *The Blue Anchor* on a Friday night, fumbling for a hankie in the darkness, on the back row amongst these bearded youths, and him the only one there with a proper tie and a jacket on.

It wasn't Lucy in the boat that sparked the tears. It was the old actor playing Krapp, his voice. His voice, his song - hardly call it a song, more of a croon - it cut Frank to the soul.

Now the day is o-ver
Night is drawing nigh
Shadows of the eve-ning
Steal a-cross the sky.

The last thing Frank remembered was Krapp saying he once had fire, *fire,* inside him, and asking, would he want it back? And once more Frank wanted to scream - *'Yes! YES! COURSE YOU BLOODY WOULD!'*

Then the play ended with the tape recorder spinning round and round, round and round, and no voice this time, just nothing. It seemed a very short play to Frank, for so much experience.

He couldn't applaud. He let 49 youngsters do it for him. Had he not been on the end seat, he wouldn't have moved at all. The audience eased past him and he was last to leave. The girl in black was waiting at the exit with a cardboard box, like a collection plate at church. He pulled a fiver from his jacket and dropped it in, amongst mostly coin.

'You liked it?' asked the girl, surprised.

'It got going. Eventually,' he sniffed.

'It's those old reels of tape' she said. 'Finding the right one, threading it, playing it.'

'Aye. Memories.'

She nodded in agreement, and Frank wanted to grab

her by the shoulders, and shake her till she bled. *What's she nodding for? What does she know about memories? She's not old enough for memories! What is she, twenty, twenty-one? Bloody hell!*

The girl in black didn't notice. 'Krapp needs them, doesn't he?' she said. 'The tapes, the memories? Yet at the same time, they're torture. Don't you think?'

Frank did think. Frank knew. Backwards.

'We've all been something,' was all he managed to say. 'Known someone.'

She nodded again. 'Mm. 'Been something. Known someone.' Yes, interesting line...'

Pause. Silence. Like in the play.

'We're here every Friday, you know. Maybe see you next week?'

He hesitated.

It's all those bloody pauses, Frank, on that stage!

'What's on?' he asked. 'Next week.'

'A play called 'Rockaby'. An old woman in a rocking chair, looking back over her life.' She shrugged an apology. 'It's another Samuel Beckett.'

An old woman, looking back over her life? More memories? More torture? Forward and back, forward and back? Is that what you need, Frank?

He turned to stare at the long thin theatre, once *The Blue Anchor's* skittle-alley.

Maybe you do, Frank. Memories are what you've been.

'*Beck*ett? I thought it said Bu- I tell you what, if you promise me a good view, like tonight, I might be persuaded.'

'I promise,' she said. 'I know you'll like it. We believe in using pubs, you see, village halls too. We believe in taking plays to ordinary people.' She stopped, awkward.

He said it for her. 'Ordinary people like me, you mean?'

See, Frank, you can be frank when you put your mind to it.

'You've a greasy ladder to climb, then, and that's a fact.'

In the half-dark, she looked squarely at him, black T-shirt and jeans appraising jacket and tie. A slight twitch flickered her lips. He thought there might be tears.

'We all have dreams', she said, in the quietest voice he'd ever heard. 'I'd rather dream than drift, any day.' She pressed her lips together to control the twitch, but it continued. 'What's wrong with having dreams?' she asked.

Another pause, another silence, like in the play.

Say something, Frank, or cry she will.

Pointing to the little stage, he said, 'Bit dark, down there. You could do with more light, at the sharp end.'

The girl in black found her voice again. 'Yes. Our techie says there's not enough power.'

'He's half right. Plenty of power coming *in*. Tell you how I know. I did the wiring when this place was a skittle-alley.' He waved at the box of tricks on the wall. 'Just needs re-jigging, that junction. Cheap as chips to do.'

'Oh. Well. You could talk to our techie? Show him what you mean? Um...if you like?'

Frank dipped his head, a probably-nod. 'Might do', he said. 'I worked on it once. Expect I could work on it twice.'

She nodded back. They stepped out of the long thin dark theatre, into evening sun.

A pause. A silence.

'So. You used to be an electrician?'

'We've all been something,' he said.

'Known someone', she added, teasing.

Pause. Silence.

Yes, Frank Smith. And you might as well remember.

Sleepless in Southampton

Put that book down, Lydia! her voice said.

And switch off the lamp, please, said her other voice.

She did.

The bedside clock glared at her, bright as a searchlight. Every sixty seconds the LED display flashed forward, with an audible click.

Click!

04.16, it said.

Everything else in the room was dark.

Including Lydia.

In the glow, she could make out brown furniture, pale green walls, cheap framed prints of ships - cruise liners mostly. Very big on cruise liners, Southampton. The half-open door to the hallway tempted her.

No. Not yet. Too early. She pulled at a loose thread on her cotton nightgown.

It was Clive who bought the clock.

I told him, it's too loud. And the numbers leave imprints on my eyeballs. He just sniffed. Clive was a sniffer. I said I want a gentle clock, that tells the time without shouting. Or sniffing.

CLICK!

04.17.

On a little notepad by the bed she'd noted when she last slept through the night. Eleven months and nineteen days. Scraps of sleep and empty acres of waking, sewn up in a patchwork quilt, that's me, she told herself. If I had a pound for every sheep I've counted, a penny for every waking thought...

Well, Liddy, what would you do with the money?

I'd buy an invisible clock!

She shuffled her toes to the bottom of the bed, to warm it up, for sleep. The bed wasn't to blame. Comfy enough. Sturdy. New mattress of memory foam.

Not called that for nothing, is it? Froth and foam, her memories. A king-sized curse of foam. And on top, a memory duvet, sealing her in like a blister pack.

What time did she go to bed? Midnight? A little after? Switched off the news, in dismay, and dozed. Till 02.04. And now it's -

Click.

04.18.

- and still awake.

Lydia did the sums in her head. Slowly, to eke out the task. Passing time. Hmph. Like in a horse race.

Time is going well on the inside but, what's this, Lydia's challenging on the outside, making ground, making ground down the home straight, and, yes, Time is faltering, with the finishing line in sight and she's edging closer, closer, closer - and she passes Time! She's the winner!

And the loser, Liddy. Waiting now, for Time to catch up…

The sums, girl. 04.18 minus 02.04 is...Two hours 14 minutes awake, waiting for the snide electric clock to -

Click!

Two hours and 15, now.

She glared at the sneery display. Digital. She'd wanted that other kind - what's it called? Anderlecht?

No, Anderlecht's a Belgian football team. Clive supported them. Clive was Belgian. Flat. Like the country. He 'followed' Anderlecht, on TV and on 'the web'. Clive worshipped technology. And football. It was Clive bought the clock.

Click.

04.20.

Not Anderlecht...*Analogue!* That's it!

Tomorrow, she told herself, I'll buy an *analogue* bedside clock, with a dial and proper hands. A gentle clock, that doesn't *CLICK* every sixty seconds like an execution. A tick is OK. Comforting. Tick-tock. Yes, an analogue clock with a quiet tick that counts the sheep for you, so you don't lie awake counting the bloody things yourself.

If the clock shops were open now, at 04.20, she could get up, wash and dress, and pop out to buy an analogue clock. If they still sell them?

Doesn't matter. The world's dark and dim at - Click, 04.21 - and the clock shops are closed.

If I close too - my eyes, that is - will I fall asleep? Maybe I'll fall asleep and never wake up. Is that what I want?

No, said her other voice. *You do NOT*.

Here we go, thought Lydia, my nightly battle of voices. What'll it be tonight?

Last night was funerals. One voice said pre-pay, the other said *just wing it.*

Previous night: stay put, or *move house*?

Before that? Get a dog, or *not*?

Oh, and horoscopes: crystal balls, or *balls*?

Stop, said her other voice. *You've done the whole list to death*. Yes, said her first voice. We've done it to death.

Silence.

Click.

04.23.

Running out of battles, the voices said. Running out.

That's what frightens me, said Lydia to the empty room.

She stared at the clock in silence till another *click* pierced her.

04.26.

With reluctance, the voices fell back on football.

Clive swore he could've turned professional. *I've got silky midfield skills*, he used to say. With a sniff. Lydia never understood what silk had to do with it. And as for 4-2-4, it sounded to her more like the time on this bloody digital clock!

She couldn't remember exactly when Clive started 'to pick up injuries'. Muscle tears. God save us, a groin strain too. Ligament damage. A fracture. *Haven't played for two years*, he'd moan. *A silky left foot like mine, going to waste.* Then it was five years, eight, twelve. Twenty. No football now, just drink. And all the while the numbers on his bathroom scales going up, up. Clive bought the scales.

Digital.

Like this bloody clock, clicking on, on.

Then Clive couldn't even click, let alone 'ghost into the penalty box', whatever that means. He certainly stopped ghosting into mine, she remembered. Wouldn't even take me to the shops. Well, in fairness, couldn't. Couldn't drive. Could barely sniff. Before long, couldn't walk. And then he couldn't even get himself to the loo.

I had to take him, at the end.

I'm not having anyone do that for me.

I'm not.

*

Click!

05.15.

Lydia must have nodded off. A good half hour in dreamland. Except she didn't dream anymore. She'd put a stop to it. Too many ghouls and ghosts, in dreams. Deal with the sods when you're wide awake, Liddy. Help pass the time.

Should she get up? Do the all-night Tesco's like young folk, in their pyjamas? No. Retain a bit of dignity. Probably get mugged on the way back. Or the way there.

She switched on the bedside lamp.

Sometimes, she switched it on just to piss off Clive's clock, take it down a peg or two. Bedtime reading stared up at her. 'Self-Help for the Sleepless', by an author she'd never heard of, Claudette Moon. On the back cover, the author's mug-shot showed a curly-haired woman in Psychologist specs, smiling winningly from blue-green eyes.

I'd be more convinced if Claudette Moon had her eyes *closed*, thought Lydia, turning to chapter five.

Never 'just lie there', advised Claudette. Instead, get out of bed and seize the day. Then another word: *optimise*. Lydia had looked it up. Make things perfect, or somesuch. Go on, optimise your time, Liddy!

She'd tried. Often.

Get up, do the crossword.

Get up, watch nightshift TV.

Get up, write notes for her memoirs on the notepad. And throw them away again.

Get up, and read.

Why? Twice as comfy reading in bed, propped up on four pillows. Two of your own - and the two that used to be Clive's.

As for doing housework at 5am…huh, be nothing left to do by midday. She slammed the book closed.

Click.

05.18.

With a groan, she opened the book again. Get up, make herbal tea, advised Claudette.

Lydia had tried that too. Elderflower and mango. Chamomile and mint. Fennel and sweet cicely. Sounded different; tasted the same. Like she was drinking her own tears.

At least in bed you save electricity.

Click.

05.19.

She flicked forward, to chapter six, 'The Dark Night of

the Soul'. 'What to do if the dark night of the soul descends', said the heading.

It's already descended! she shouted, waving the book at the empty bedroom. *It's here! I could write the chapter myself! I don't need you!*

Read, said her other voice. *Better than staring at the clock.*

'Revisit the golden moments in your life,' advised Claudette. 'Your finest memories, your proudest achievements.' The book called them *golden moments*. Re-visit your top ten - your top ten golden moments - write them down. 'Give your self-esteem a joy-injection!' said the book.

Lydia baulked at the *ten*, but had a go.

She struggled to get two. Half way, she hankered for a *golden moment* with Robert Redford, a proper joy-injection for her self-esteem. But even Robert Redford's growing old.

She swapped the book for her pen and notepad.

Golden Moment Number One, she wrote. Coming first in Maths, at school, aged nine. She won a prize, a book about astronomy. And been star-gazing ever since, Liddy. At Prizegiving, The Lady Mayoress did the honours. The school invited a different public figure - a *Dignitary* - every year. Lydia got The Lady Mayoress, Mrs Berryborough, a thin, toothy woman in a frock made from old curtains, her chain so heavy it pulled her spindly neck down towards the ground. She's under it now, of course.

Golden Moment Number Two. Age ten, at the seaside with mum, before she died and himself buggered off with a floosy. Morecombe, it was. Gran took her in, till age 18, then Gran buggered off too, her duty done, poor soul. Incidentally - or is it coincidentally? - Gran ended up in the same graveyard as The Lady Mayoress, so there's a connection at least.

Click.

05.21.

Golden Moment Number Three... Would that be Clive?

No.

No, it wouldn't.

Clive wanted to move to Belgium, but Lydia refused. Lonely enough in *England.* To compensate, Clive played football, and after the pubs closed he trundled his beery breath onto a memory-foam mattress warmed by the heat of her body, and fell asleep. With a sniff. The clicky search-light clock never bothered *him.*

Lydia's role was to lie there, wondering why she was lying there. And to shop, clean, cook, listen. Listen to Clive sniffing on about football, Belgium, pubs. If they had holidays, she must have blinked.

It was Clive who dragged them to Southampton. For a job on the cruise liners, he told her. Might get a free cruise out of it, she thought. Turned out, maintenance men never went to sea. Once or twice he crawled up and down The Solent, to test repairs, but she never got an invite. Seaside life should be romantic, but they lived by the Docks. Gantries and cranes. Foreheads of ships like the top tiers of big white wedding cakes, dwarfing you.

Her wedding cake was a tatty little blob.

Clive used to climb aboard one cruise-liner after another, mend things - she never understood what - then climb off again.

I don't climb off, he sniffed, *I disembark.*

Tuh, the glamour of it.

No, Clive would only sneak in at Number Three as...what? A ticket? An entry ticket, to a café, to the annual Christmas party at The Docks, or once a blue moon to the pictures. The places you don't want to sit in on your own.

Which is what she mostly did now.

Click.

05.42.

Must have dozed - for which, Lord, etcetera. 'Self-Help for the Sleepless' still lay in her lap, still urging her to write down her Top Ten Golden Moments. She swapped the book for her notepad, and scoured an empty past.

All she conjured up was Pitch-Dark Moment Number One.

It was after she left school, at sixteen, with her Careers Teacher's blessing, to work in the office at Arrowby's, Modern Appliances for Modern Homes.

'I won a prize for Maths', she said, at the interview.

She didn't tell them the prize was a book on astronomy. Didn't say she'd star-gazed ever since. They were supposed to train her as an accountant, pay for her to qualify. All she did was add up numbers, day after day, and scratch the totals in a ledger. When Arrowby's went bust, she did the same for Portaloos Ltd, then for the Council, till she got rationalised. Then for Drome's, who made nuts and bolts.

Pitch-Dark Moment Number One happened on the bus to Drome's, one cloudless autumn morning. She stared through the window at the empty sky - could see it now - and thought of dusk falling. And she knew, in her soul, that when darkness came, if there were any stars at all they would be far away, too far, and she would never be able to see them.

'Yours will be a tiny life, Liddy', she heard her own young voice murmur. 'The Wicked Witch of Tiny Lives has touched you with her wand. Tiny, you. Tiny you will remain.'

She threw down the notepad. *Shouldn't have listened to yourself, you silly cow!*

Clive's was a tiny life too. She thought she'd be safe inside it, a reflection inside a mirror, so she listened to the sniff of his tiny voice. And married him.

*

06.13.

Must've dozed again.

Her fingers found the notepad, and she wondered should she write down Pitch-Dark Moment Number One? Record it, to re-live it? Give her self-esteem a joy-injection?

No, her other voice said.

Voice and clock, between them, made up her mind.

CLICK!

06.14.

To Lydia, the click was a sniff.

SNIFF!

A sniff-click.

A tiny-life, dead-end sniff-click.

A Clive sniff-click.

No. No more.

SHUT UP! she yelled, at the clock. And pushing the duvet aside, she swung her legs out of bed, reached down and yanked the plug from its socket. And clambered back.

The clock faded to a sniffless, numberless silence. Might have to *guess* the time now, Liddy.

Or not bother, said her other voice.

Grabbing the notepad, in the white space next to Golden Moment Number Three she scribbled, *A Day with Robert Redford*. Then she scrubbed out *Day*, and added *Night*. If you're reduced to inventing the past, Liddy, don't make it tiny. Or clean.

Recharged, her pen scratched Golden Moment Number Four onto the page - *A Cruise*. They do cruises for Singles, don't they? A short one to start with - The Canary Islands. She'd never been - never been much of anywhere.

But, Liddy, calling it a Golden Moment, when it hasn't happened yet? Is that allowed?

Who cares? said her voice.

She had the insurance money, from when Clive died. Plenty of travel agents in Southampton, and even a booking office near the Docks. Perhaps Robert Redford would tap romantic knuckles on her cabin door, and have the stamina for a second sleepless night with lovely Liddy?

Golden Moment Number Five gave her pause.

A visit to a Telescope? At night? To star-gaze? She'd never even squinted up a telescope. Or is it down? What was that place called, with the massive dish? Jodhpurs Bank?

Or sell the house, move away from the docks? Yes, what a true golden moment that would be, a smaller house for a bigger life. Ordinary, but bigger than the one so far.

And, someone ordinary like me, could I really write my memoirs?

Yes, Liddy, why not? They don't have to be for anyone else.

She was truly tired. She glanced at the clock.

Blank.

More Golden Moments tomorrow, she said, reaching for the light switch.

Wait, Liddy. One more first, nudged her other voice.

Under Golden Moment Number Five, she wrote: *New clock. Analogue. With a dial and proper hands. And a gentle tick.*

Lydia dropped the notepad in the bedside drawer, and switched off the light.

At Yeovilton Weir

Maeve gazed at unstoppable water swilling over the weir, hissing, beating. Drops of spray flickered through sunlight, forming brief rainbows before the river re-claimed them. Near the bank, darker water pooled languidly back on itself, away from the white swirl of the falls. Faint trails of slime coloured the stream. She watched broken branches twist in a black sludge that was clear water when she and Jack first came here, in 1962.

She should never have looked up 'chronic' in the dictionary. Because the doctors were telling the truth. Jack's Alzheimer's *had* 'worsened with time', not that he was aware of it.

Yesterday, she'd persuaded him into the car, and coaxed him onto the promenade at Lyme Regis, but no further. Her Jack sat on a low wall by the beach, staring at the blue tide, at fishing boats in the lee of the Cobb, at the pale distant bump of Golden Cap, and uttering not a word of recognition.

Tomorrow, she'd drive them to another memory - the long commanding ridge by Cadbury Castle, where once they'd rested on an old stone seat to gaze at magnificence. Jack said it was the finest view in England. Perhaps too steep for him now.

Today, was Yeovilton Weir. The pair of them sat on a solitary bench by the river, listening to the swish of spray.

Even before she sat, she was cursing her own slow mind. Sea walls, stone seats, a wooden bench. Her plan for re-visiting happier times had a common denominator, but it wasn't memory. It was benches. She was choosing places where Jack could sit. Lord knows, where she could too. Tired, they were both tired. He from disease. She, from dealing with it.

Jack first brought her here in the heady, defiant summer of 1962...

*

'Why are we stopping, Jack?'

He'd pulled the Hillman Imp into the verge, by Yeovilton Weir, and was looking ahead, behind and around.

'Is someone following us?' she asked, confused.

'Don't be daft, Maeve,' he chuckled. 'Have you got your Sunday knickers on?'

Misunderstanding his intentions, she gave him a playful swipe. They'd made love in the tiny Hillman Imp before, but it was a challenge. 'No fancy stuff,' he'd said. 'Not till we can afford a bigger car.'

Or a house, she'd thought. Another year, as it turned out, before they scraped enough for the deposit on a little hamstone cottage at the foot of Ham Hill.

The last time they tried the Hillman Imp sex-challenge, they were parked in shade, in dense woodland. Today was sun-bright, one of the few dry days this August, and the car already an oven.

'Sunday knickers or not, Jack, it's a bit...public here. Can't we pull off the road where the trees are thicker. Where there's some shade?'

'Cuh,' he laughed. You're hornier than I am. Not the car, you dilly. The water!'

He pointed to the white-diamond-sparkle of the weir, and unbuttoned his shirt.

'But it's dangerous, Jack, with all the rain. And what if someone sees us?'

'First answer: I'll save you. Second answer: leave your Sunday drawers on!'

Maeve laughed. Flouting common sense was a fine freedom. She stripped down to her Marks and Spencer's underwear, giggled at Jack's cod body-builder pose, and snapped the elastic of his Y-fronts.

'Ow!' he said, and chased her to the weir. No Health and Safety, no Risk Assessment, just the briefest check for voyeurs before they sprinted through sticky evening heat and splashed, all a-giggle, into wonderful, dangerous water...

*

It was different today, the weir. In 1962, a thin walkway connected the riverbanks. Anyone bold enough could freely straddle the tumbling cascade, and dance from one bank to the other. Jack had done precisely that, in his Y-fronts heavy with water.

‘They’ll fall down!’ she shouted, with her last grain of decorum.

‘Later!’ he laughed back at her.

And, yes, she remembered, he’d kept his word.

The walkway was gone now, and a sluice-gate cut the weir in two. A modest waterfall splashed into the river. Jack was gazing at it, his brows squeezing and straightening in a forehead-dance she’d grown used to.

This was Jack’s first face, where, often enough, he remembered a grain of the past and found the right words to say so.

His second face was a now-familiar glaze, empty and flat, freezing his features for minutes on end. Or longer.

For Maeve, Jack’s third face was the worst - a calmer remembering face when a memory returned, curling his lips into a smile and filling his eyes with laughter. Sometimes he nodded his head in happy confirmation. Maeve loved his third face.

And hated it. Because though memory filled him, he could find no words to describe it, and she was locked outside like a dog with muddy paws, waiting for an unknown hand to switch on the freezing water and hose her down.

*

They kept a pair of towels in the Hillman’s tiny boot, and dried themselves by the car, smiling and kissing. No other cars went by, no dogs, no people. Maeve remembered only laughter and the waterfall’s song.

Once dressed, they wandered back to the weir, lazing on their bench, listening in silence as the gush of water sang in a language of its own. Together, they watched the silver droplets fly and fall, fly and fall, and heard the faint bright notes of a blackbird.

Maeve could still remember the warmth of her flesh after the water's chill. And Jack's warmth too, pressed against her.

Their warmth remained, even when the sun became the moon, and they drove away.

*

Jack stared at the weir, at the confusion of streams, the flow from above meeting the flow below, and intertwining, twisting, slowing, and turning back on itself.

'Water,' he said.

Experienced now, Maeve drew a bottle from her coat and unscrewed the top. He pushed it aside.

'*Water*,' he repeated, his hand flicking at the weir-pool below.

'Yes, Jack. Yeovilton Weir. Remember? You brought me here. August, 1962.'

Jack's shoulders jerked in a shrug of pointlessness. Even yesterday's date was beyond him.

'We parked just there, Jack, where the car is now.' They had an SUV, not a Hillman Imp, with a boot big enough to carry the entire household of Jack's needs.

'The car,' he said, creaking up from the bench and wandering over to the SUV.

She followed.

That's what I do now, she thought. I follow. I pretend to lead, but what I do is follow. Follow Jack to our car. Follow Jack to our house. Follow Jack to an unknown land of maybe-sleep, or maybe-not.

Jack stared back at the weir. At the car. At the weir. As she watched, his remembering face appeared, lips curling to a smile, eyes laughing, head nodding in confirmation. Once again, Maeve loved it, and hated it.

Joy, the patience-of-a-saint in the making, was to see his memory smiling at the water.

Pain would follow, she knew, when Jack's memory delivered no words for sharing, no life-language, and Maeve was locked outside.

At least Jack was laughing, if a low chuckle can be called a laugh.

His laugh grew louder, chuckle becoming cackle, and she stared at him, eyes wide. A younger Jack began to bang his hand on the bonnet of the SUV, a waterfall of hoots and belly-laughs tumbling out of him, tumbling past the sluice-gate of his memory, in a brief white-diamond-sparkle of spray.

Maeve had no words. She could only gaze at her guffawing, glad-laughing old Jack.

'*Are...?*' He could barely speak, but for laughter now.

'*Are your ...?*' His hand beat the car bonnet as he tried to control himself.

'*Are your Sunday knickers clean, Maeve?*' he managed to chuckle out, before manic laughter returned.

Her smile as wide as a lifetime, Maeve opened the passenger door and eased him in.

'If you laugh any harder, Jack, *yours* won't be!'

The car shook, all journey home, with remembered, skinny-dip laughter from August, 1962.

To the reader

If you've enjoyed these stories, please consider leaving a review on Amazon.co.uk, Amazon.com, or Goodreads.

And why not try my crime mystery series, with Detective Inspector Zig Batten and his team, set in the apple-orchard landscape of the West of England?

For a taste of Zig and his sidekick Sergeant Ball, here's a free bonus story about Batten's early days as a keen but green Detective Constable…

Inspector Batten's New Moustache

Sergeant Ball's throat opened like a wound, and a healing pint of cider disappeared. With a single flick of his empty glass, he reeled in the barman.

Inspector Zig Batten's own golden pint was almost full. He sat easy at The Jug and Bottle's apple-wood bar, watching Ball's now familiar cider ritual. Only once had he kept pace with his off-duty Sergeant and, next day, the hangover from hell re-educated him.

'It's a sponge, zor.' Ball's Somerset twang couldn't manage 'sir'.

'What is? Your throat?'

'No. Your moustache.' Ball jabbed a sausage finger at Batten's top-lip. 'More cider there than in your glass.'

Batten ran a finger over his wet moustache.

'Shave it off, zor. It's stopping the cider going where it belongs.'

'Not bloody likely.' He gave his moustache another wipe. 'It's new, is this.'

Ball's ginger smile disagreed. 'New? Doesn't look new.'

'New shape, Ballie. Previous one was one of these.'

Batten demonstrated, index finger and thumb flicking down from lips to chin, in a Zapata shape.

‘What, you had one of those Mexican moustaches? You?’

‘Yorkshire-Mexican. I was young. All the rage in Leeds, back then, a long Zapata moustache. Retro.’

‘All the rage with the ladies?’

‘Did me no harm.’

‘Bit daft you shaving the ends off, then.’

‘Who says I did?’

‘Well, someone must’ve.’

‘It’s a bit of a story.’

Ball’s second pint arrived.

‘Not going anywhere,’ he said…

*

Brand-new to CID back then, lowly Detective Constable Batten was gobsmacked to be part of the big raid.

‘Must be a staff shortage,’ said Ged Morley, best pal and fellow DC.

Whatever the reason, in the van went Zig and Ged. Batten’s toes tingled in the presence of crime, and his nervous feet tap-tap-tapped, till Inspector Farrar told him to park his shoes up his arse or he’d do it for him.

The stake-out was silent, disciplined. A warehouse, chock-full of perfume, luxury goods, designer clothing. They’d been chasing the gang of top-end thieves for weeks.

‘Pint of Tetley’s says I nab one of the sods before you do, Zig,’ whispered Ged.

‘Done’, Batten whispered back. His quick frame was gangly, but could squash a crook.

When it all kicked off, Zig treated Ged to an elbow and sped from the van before his pal could recover. About to flatten what the case-notes called 'Suspect 2', he tripped on his over-keen size-nines and flattened himself instead. Where the knees of his trousers used to be, two jagged holes stared up like bloodshot eyes. Ged sailed past and laid out the fleeing crook.

'Another pint of Tetley's in the kitty, Zig,' said Ged.

'Ow!' said Batten, dabbing torn flesh.

Ragged at the knees, a young DC Batten tried hard to look suave during the post-raid grilling. No question of nipping home for a change of trousers, with five crooks to gut.

D.I. Farrar dubbed the unknown Number Six 'Mr Brain - 'because he's the only bugger from this lot who's got one.' The Mastermind proved Farrar right by being too canny to show up, or tell his crew his real name. Instead, the captive five got the hair-dryer.

'Make it easy on yourself. Just confirm what we know about your nameless boss,' Batten lied to Suspect 2. 'Sixty-odd, right? Tall, Fair. Er, clean-shaven. Sloppy dresser. That him?'

'Huh', said Suspect 2. 'Try forty, and five-foot bugger-all. Salt and pepper hair, as it happens, and long. And he dresses like a toff - a bearded toff.' Suspect 2 stared with contempt at Batten's torn knees. 'No holes in *his* trousers.'

When a squashed Batten reported this assumed pack of lies to Farrar, the Inspector's face lit up.

'Progress, Zig. That's four of 'em now, description same

or similar, and no conferring. We can discount the comedian in there.'

The nearest cell door boomed as Farrar gave it a mighty kick.

'According to him, Mr Brain's real name's Winston Churchill, and he swans round in a gorilla suit and a green wig!'

The cell door boomed in response to a second kick.

'I don't care if his real name's Churchill, Stalin or Roosevelt,' Farrar told his team. 'We're looking for a short-arse with long salt and pepper hair - and a beard to match. 'So, fingers out and eyes open, all of you!'

Farrar's face screwed itself into a knot.

'Hey, Zig. What the bloody hell *is* salt and pepper hair, when it's at home?'

Post-raid celebrations began mid-evening, in a private room above The Victoria, fittingly close to the City of Leeds Law Courts. The drinking seemed never to end. Not since his student days had Batten seen so much booze downed in a single night. And the more it flowed, the more stick he took for his ripped knees.

'Air vents, are they?'

'You must be low-slung, to need a zip-fly there!'

Even the fair-minded Inspector Farrar asked to see Batten's C.I. Knee card, before sliding a pint and a whisky chaser across the table.

'Don't worry, Zig', he said, pointing his empty glass at the rest of the team. 'It's their way of saying 'welcome'. You were too quick and fell over. Forget it. Move on. Some of this lot, they can't even fall over slowly.'

By midnight, it was Batten who'd fallen over, from compensatory drink. The 'team' did the decent thing and ferried him home

Next morning found him spread-eagled on his sitting room sofa, twin mounds of a lacy pink D-cup bra clipped across the knee-holes in the trousers he still wore. Whose bra, why pink, and how it got there he had no idea. Head like a breezeblock, he shed his broken trousers, flung the D-cups across the room, and flopped to the loo. The bathroom mirror revealed a car-wreck, with a grey face attached. Peering closer, he recognised it.

Ten tired fingers pressed and prodded his features, checking they were all still there.

They weren't!

Lop-sided, his face.

'I'm having a stroke!' he told the mirror.

No, said the mirror. *Look closer.*

He did.

'Bastards!'

To the right of his mouth, the Yorkshire-Mexican moustache bristled down towards his chin. To the left, it was sawn off at his top lip.

His fingers prodded the strip of bare flesh, dry-shaved by persons unknown while a befuddled Batten snored. It would have been baby-bottom-white, but for a long scar of razor burn - scarlet, hot - cackling at Batten from the mirror.

*

Ball's chuckles were seismic.

'Your lot stitched you up, good and proper.'

'Ta for the sympathy, Ballie. Razor burn's bloody painful.'

'Apologies, zor. But, you, a lop-sided Zapata. Can't get the image out of my head.'

'Oh, drink your cider.'

Ball needed no invitation. One long swallow and he flicked a second empty glass at the barman.

'Must've tingled all the way down to your toes, zor, when you splashed on the Old Spice?'

'Sod that. Went down the chemist shop, for some cream to rub on. I had a face like a slapped behind.'

*

'I think...let me see...this product would be best for your... predicament, sir. It's a soothing balm. A gel.'

After an age, the chemist produced a white tube of something. Batten wondered if it worked on knees.

'Soothing and healing, sir. Treats the symptoms, cures the cause.'

The chemist twirled a discreet finger at the red landing-strip scarring one side of Batten's face, then at the delicate pale-pink version on the other. All in his own good time.

A hungover Batten failed to understand how a trained chemist, whose name-badge said he was Mr Swift, could take so bloody long to lift a tube of gumph off a shelf, shove it in a paper bag and tippety-tap his fingers on a till. As stimulation, Batten semaphored with his wallet.

Mr Swift, though, was Batten's nightmare: a talker.

'Isn't life strange, sir? You're the second one this morning.'

'Second what?' asked Batten, toe-tapping the vinyl floor.

'Well. What may I call it? Second shaving incident? The previous chappie, mind, his face was Mount Etna to your little firework.'

Batten's glower said, 'hand over the gel, and *stop talking*!'

Mr Swift, inept at reading faces, babbled on.

'Razor burn *invading* his cheeks, chap before you. Never seen a worse example. Goodness, what was he thinking? His whiskers had been scythed away in record time. To match the awful haircut, I imagine. A jumping bean, the little chap.'

Batten knew how he felt. 'How much?' he said.

'How much hair?'

'No! How much for *that*?' He shook a claw at the tube of gel, still glued to the chemist's hand.

'Apologies, sir, apologies. I thought you were enquiring about his hair, the previous chap. It was short, you see. Very shor - '

'Look, can I pay for this and be on my way?'

'I do beg your pardon, sir. Of course, of course.' He reached for a paper bag, and tickled a code into the till. Talking all the while.

'We meet every type here, naturally. But when a chap

comes in, razor burn aflame on his cheeks, haircut done by an untrained chimpanzee, well…'

Zig, can you arrest a chemist for Grievous Bodily Talking?

'You and I, sir, would we patronise a hairdressing salon where untrained chimpanzees wield scissors? I think not. And dare I even call it a 'salon'? 'Scene of the crime', more like, hah-hah.'

Batten's chin burnt. His hangover boomed inside his skull in frustration. But his brain sat up like a guard dog when the chemist mentioned 'crime'.

'Did you say short hair?'

'This long, sir.' He held up a finger and thumb, an inch apart. 'Snipped off by a chimpanzee. Perhaps an inverted-snobbery take on the Bohemian look? Given how expensively-dressed he was.'

'Expensive?'

'Beyond the wallets of you and I, sir. Not that it's my place to presume, of course'. He shook apologetic fingers at Batten's workaday plain-clothes.

Should've seen me an hour ago, thought Batten. Ripped trousers and a lacy D-cup bra.

'What colour was it?'

'Colour?'

Is this tosser going to repeat everything I say?

'His hair. What colour?'

'Very little hair to be seen, sir. As I said. Before.'

Mr Swift felt the jab of a Batten eyebrow.

'Oh, black and white, I suppose. Salt and pepper, isn't that what it's called?'

The hangover-throb became a tingle in Batten's toes.

'How did he pay?'

'Pay?'

A second eyebrow pierced Mr Swift. The chemist threw one back.

'It was a tube of gel, not the Crown Jewels. He paid in coins. From-his-pock-et.'

Batten couldn't decide whether to slap his own forehead, or Mr Swift's.

Blast! No numbered banknotes. No credit card trail.

Looking up at the ceiling, he asked, 'any CCTV in here?'

'Whether yea or nay, sir, we wouldn't care to advertise.'

Batten dragged out his warrant card.

'In which case, yes. We're a chemist shop. We store drugs.'

He pointed above him, at a light fitting. Batten saw only a light fitting. Hidden camera.

'Was it on, the camera? When the salt and pepper man came in?'

'It is permanently on. Except when broken. Which it isn't.'

'Tapes? You keep them, I hope?'

'Obliged to. Sir.'

Had Mr Swift not swiftly left the storeroom where the CCTV monitor lived, he might never have left at all. When Batten viewed the tape he ached for a scapegoat. The camera was set too high, its focus too narrow. All the tape showed was the tip of a nose and the top of an ugly salt-and pepper haircut. The haircut, in turn, sat above a five-foot well-dressed short-arse. No hint of a mug-shot. And expensive clothing is easy to dump.

The black and white hair might have clinched it - had the tape been in colour. But everything visible was black and white, short-arse's hair included. In court, a defence lawyer could claim its true hue was green ginger and oatmeal, and get away with it.

Batten wrote a receipt for the video-tape, his pen gouging angry deep furrows in the chit. He could do nothing more than gather up the shards of his broken demeanour, and report in.

Once he'd escaped from Mr Swift's Talk-Emporium, that is.

'I'm so sorry I could not help you, sir. But coins it was, and the camera is where it is.' The chemist tapped a finger on the useless video-tape. 'As you have seen.'

DC Batten glared.

'Of course, he did use a credit card for the other purchase.'

DC Batten froze.

'What other purchase? You never mentioned another purchase!'

'You never asked. Sir.'

The fateful gap between training and experience punched its way into Batten's memory. It would live there, a corrective note, forever. He back-pedalled, smiling as sincerely as rank hypocrisy would allow.

'Fine. So, Mr Salt-and-Pepper-Hair, he bought…what?'

Mr Swift-the-Chemist decided to work against type - by saying nothing. Instead, he pointed to a display of travel accessories against the shop's far wall. Batten stared at travel irons, continental plug adaptors, luggage scales. No surprise. Leeds and Bradford Airport was five miles down the road.

Tingling toes rattled like a drumroll now.

He followed the chemist's moving finger purely from détente, having already homed in on a rack of cabin bags, the perfect size for a plane's overhead locker. Where it would always be in sight of its owner. As he, and it, left the country.

'What colour?'

'Hair, sir? Salt and pepper. As previously mentioned.'

Batten pretended to return the smug smile.

'No. Cabin bag.'

'Black, sir. As you can see, we stock only black and mauve. Gender preference, I expect?'

Huh, offender preference, thought Batten, wondering why an absconding five-foot-short-arse, with a chimpanzee-haircut, didn't pay in anonymous cash.

'Credit card? You sure?'

Wordlessly, Swift stepped over to the till, tickled in a code, and with a conjuror's aplomb produced a carbon flimsy. The card belonged to a Jeremy Puckleton. It looked genuine - with juicy traceable numbers to kick-start a hunt. Batten mumbled humble thanks, and wrote a second receipt.

His false display of gratitude had a mixed blessing. It unlocked the chemist's tongue.

‘Now I come to think of it, your salt and pepper man wanted to know where was the nearest bank. Three miles away, I told him. Our suburb is not thought significant enough to warrant a branch nearby. I mentioned this too. He seemed uninterested.’

Mr Swift gave Batten a look.

‘All he did was stare at his watch. Much as you are doing now, sir. Stared, coldly, as if it was a calculator and he had sums to do. And then, presto, out comes his credit card. I surmise he carried insufficient cash to pay for the cabin bag, insufficient time to visit a bank, and had an imminent aeroplane to catch. No?’

Batten ignored Mr Swift’s final flourish. Nor was he going to say, ‘what a clever Detective-Chemist you are.’ Instead, he checked the transaction time. Jeremy Puckleton had shaved off salt-and-pepper beard and hair in a panic, used a traceable credit card to buy a cabin bag, and headed from this very shop to the likely escape route of Leeds and Bradford Airport - less than half an hour ago.

Before Mr Swift’s tongue could unleash more words, Batten was sprinting to his car-radio.

Sore knees were history.

A tube of soothing gel lay forgotten on the Chemist’s counter.

*

Sergeant Ball’s off-duty glass had been empty for six minutes - a record.

'You got him? Mr Brain? At the airport?'

'*I* didn't. I just got his real name and a new description. Speeded things up, though. And earned me plenty of brownie points. He was doing a runner with the laundered proceeds. Bloody cabin bag was chock-full of bearer bonds. Won them playing poker, he claimed.'

'Huh, original. What'd he get? Six years?'

'Eight. Got two extra for the crap haircut.'

Sergeant Ball's chuckles became the sound of sausage fingers tapping an empty glass.

'Right. My shout', said his Inspector.

Batten headed for the now-busy bar, but decided to keep part of the story to himself…

*

D.I. Farrar had already alerted security at relevant air and ferry ports, well before a green Detective Constable entered Mr Swift's Talk-Emporium. Checking manifests for a name like Jeremy Puckleton did make Farrar's life easier. But regardless of Batten's intervention, every forty-something five-foot male traveller would have got the once-over, whether bald, bearded, blonde, clean-shaven or dressed in a sack.

A week later, the CID team bustled into the same private room above The Victoria, for a second celebratory piss-up. So many meaty hands slapped Batten on the back he was coming out in bruises. He slid a pint and a whisky chaser across the table to D.I. Farrar, and lowered his voice.

'You told them it was me, sir. Didn't you?' Batten pointed to his colleagues, filling happy throats with beer and lager. 'You told them it was me who cracked the case? But we both know I didn't.'

Farrar flashed a knowing smile, and juggled a beer-mat.

'Integration, Zig. That's all. You're the new lad here.' The beer-mat tapped Batten on the knuckles, before pointing at the boisterous bar. 'This lot can't remember having to slog their way down Experience Street. They're so old they think they were never new. And you've got brains. You're educated. Makes 'em wary.'

'They've got brains too. They must know it wasn't all me.'

'Well, memory loss is a funny thing, Zig,' said Farrar, swallowing half a pint before dropping his voice. 'Make the best of tonight. Everyone needs a start. We've all been you, falling on our arses. You know, one leg keen, one cack-handed.'

Batten rubbed his knees. Painful reminders.

'Learn it, Zig. Learn it, store it, use it. You won't always get a freebie from Lady Luck.' Farrar drained his beer. 'She dropped in on you, last week.' With a flick, the whisky chaser disappeared. 'Bloody well put it to use, her visit.'

*

Batten placed a fresh pint in front of Ball. He was sticking to halves, not being blessed with a Ball-like mineshaft of a throat.

'There was a presentation after,' he told his cider-merry Sergeant. 'The whole CID team lined up, pints in the air, and I had to run the gauntlet from one end of the bar to the other. I was lucky. They still had a thirst on, so not much ale got wasted on me.'

Ball took a knee-jerk pull from his glass.

'When I got past the guard of honour, there was a parcel sitting on the bar, my name in felt-tip, and a big red ribbon tied up in a bow.'

'Let me guess. New trousers?'

'Close. I'd chucked the ripped ones in the re-cycling bin. Ged swore it wasn't him who fished them out, but there they were.'

'Not much of a present, pair of broken trousers.'

'This time, the buggers had sewn the lacy D-cups over both knees. Not great, the needlework, but functional. And where the cleavage goes, they'd bunged a massive fake moustache - I've still got it somewhere. Poking out the zip-fly was the world's largest tube of gel. For razor-burn. The sods pissed themselves at my expense.'

Ball joined them.

Batten made no mention of the team's second gift, carefully wrapped, nestling quietly in the pocket of his re-purposed trousers. When he tore it open, there were no hoots and jeers this time. His colleagues applauded, every one of them, meaning it.

A pair of antique salt-and-pepper shakers winked up at him.

Solid silver, hallmarked.

Exquisite.

He still used them.

*

‘Ever find out whose it was?’

‘Whose what?’

‘The D-cup bra. Wasn’t yours!’

Batten sipped and pondered.

‘That’s another story, Ballie. For another day.’

Ball could wait. He raised his cider.

Batten watched it disappear.

A more experienced Batten reappears in book 1, *A Killing Tree*, where he struggles with his enforced move from urban Yorkshire to not-so-sleepy Somerset. Before he can blink, hikers discover a dead body slumped against a tree on a lonely hill... www.smarturl.it/akte

A January Killing sees Batten and his new love-interest at a traditional cider 'Wassail', in a pitch-black orchard on a winter night. Celebratory shotguns are fired into the trees, to deter 'evil spirits' and spark a fresh crop of apples. But not every shotgun fires blanks, and next day it's a dead body that has blossomed in the orchard... www.smarturl.it/ajk

And keep a look out for book 3, *An Easter Killing*. The books can be read in series or stand-alone.

Acknowledgements

Huge thanks to the many pre-readers who patiently commented on early drafts of these stories, particularly Yvonne, Sam, Kitty, Gwyn, Shan, Beryl, Penny, Cynthia, Pammie, Moya, and Pete.

And once again, gratitude to all those who listened to me banging on about the damn things.

24779746R00089

Printed in Poland
by Amazon Fulfillment
Poland Sp. z o.o., Wrocław